SISTER AT ST

Jean knew that she should have kept to her
resolution to write to Blair, telling him that she
could not marry him; but though she had
begun innumerable letters, she had not been
able to bring herself to irrevocably shut the
door on her happiness. She was telling herself
now, with bitter self-contempt, that she was
inexcusably weak for allowing herself to seize
on the excuse that he was caught up in
important work, and nothing should be done
to disturb his mind at this juncture.
She had taken off her gloves, and as she
looked down at her bare hands the sun caught
the sapphire and diamonds of her engagement
ring.
An almost unbearable pain pierced her heart.
She knew that as long as she lived she would
never forget the torture of these last days,
each one of which had brought her nearer to
the decision she could not make—and yet
knew she must.

**Also by the same author,
and available in Coronet Books:**

Sister at
St. Catherine's

Hermina Black

CORONET BOOKS
Hodder and Stoughton

Copyright © 1969 by Hermina Black

First published in Great Britain 1969 by
Hodder and Stoughton Limited

Coronet Edition 1971
Second impression 1976

———————————————————————————

Printed in Great Britain for
Hodder and Stoughton Paperbacks, a
division of Hodder & Stoughton Ltd.,
Mill Road, Dunton Green, Sevenoaks,
Kent by Cox & Wyman Ltd.,
London, Reading and Fakenham

ISBN 0 340 15114 5

Chapter 1

I

Sunshine flooded through the high windows of the long ward, where the white walls bore murals of scenes from the world's best known and loved fairy tale: golden-haired Cinderella in rags, and in ball dress; sitting lonely by the fire; dancing with her Prince; flying from the chimes of midnight, and finally triumphantly fitted with the glass slipper. Those wall paintings were the work of a famous artist, who had an unfashionable belief that his gift should be used to create beauty rather than ugliness. He had painted those pictures as a thank-offering for a small, precious life, which the doctors and nurses at St. Catherine's had helped to save.

But the attention of the occupants of the two rows of white beds was claimed by something else just then, while they watched the slender, navy blue uniformed figure whom they had learnt to know as "Sister" making her way towards them.

The eyes of those children who were too ill to take much notice of their surroundings, brightened when she paused beside them to say a soft, comforting word, rearranging the bedclothes, or just smiling at them.

Cinderella was a surgical ward, and most of the present inmates were for the time being confined to their beds. Anyhow, it was the hour when those who could get up were resting with toys or books to keep them interested.

Jean Campbell was half way down the room before her Staff Nurse came from one of the curtained cubicles at the far end of it, and moved quickly to meet her.

"Everything all right, Nurse?" Jean asked, the momentary slight drawing together of her dark brows relaxing.

5

"Yes, Sister. Nothing fresh to report." And following Jean's glance towards the cubicles: "No change. He was rather restless after you first went off duty, but he's sleeping now. Summers is with him."

"He has not been left at all?" There was a crisper note in Sister's soft voice.

"Oh, no. It's – a bit awkward when we're short staffed. There should really be a special —"

"We don't need outside help. Good heavens! there are six of us . . . Mr. Marston has not been in again?"

"No."

"And the tonsillectomy?"

"She's come round. Quite normal."

"Good." Turning aside Sister paused to bend over the small drowsy patient referred to. "Did you telephone the mother as I promised?"

"Yes; thank goodness *she* doesn't want to take up her quarters here. With five others at home I suppose she's learnt to take things in her stride."

"Poor thing, I've no doubt she would rather have the child under her own eye. But I think she was fairly satisfied to leave her with us." Jean moved on, the little crease still between the arches of her brows when a minute later she passed behind the blue curtains screening the fifteenth bed in the ward. Making a warning gesture to the young nurse who was sitting beside the bed, she stood looking down at the child who lay in it.

"Has he been restless?" she asked softly.

"Not very, Sister. Pulse good, temperature slightly below normal, breathing good. I've kept the drip going." The young nurse was eager to sound very professional. "Mr. Marston said we were to —"

"Yes, yes. Go and get your tea now, Summers. I will stay with him until you come back."

"Yes, Sister." Nurse Summers rose, then, a hand on the curtain, hesitated.

"Yes?" Jean looked round enquiringly.

"Only — he opened his eyes once, Sister. I think he was looking for you." Summers, the youngest of the three

6

student nurses on the ward, was still inexperienced enough to colour shyly. "It—seemed as though he wanted someone, and he has clung to you so much since he came in."

"He won't be remembering anyone yet. Run along now," Jean said kindly. And not realizing how devastatingly another Sister might have snubbed her, Summers went happily off, thinking what a dear Sister Campbell was, and more than on the brink of heroine-worship!

Poor wee laddie! thought Jean, taking the vacant chair, and gently replacing the little hands which had suddenly emerged from under the sheets. The clenched fingers relaxed, twining about her own, and though her serene expression remained unchanged, a stab of pain contracted her heart. She had learnt long ago to control any strong emotion where her young charges were concerned; above all never to show how intensely some of the cases which passed through her hands affected her. To do that would be only to weaken herself and rouse an undesirable reaction in her patients; one had to learn to be as calm and impersonal as possible in a job like hers; to remember what an astringent Sister had told her during her training: "You are here to heal, not to weep over the patients!"

It was nearly a year now since Jean, Staff Nurse on Cinderella for two years previously, had been promoted to her present position of authority. There had been some heartburning at the time for those who considered they should have had priority for the vacancy, which had occurred when the former Sister had left to get married. But today there was hardly a member of the nursing staff who would not have applauded Matron's arbitrary choice.

It was because of her rigid self-control that Jean had become the magnificent nurse she was. Nevertheless, she could not help growing fonder of certain children, and from the first moment when she and six-year-old Timothy Barrington met, there had been a swift "love affair" between them. But then everyone on the ward, and many outside it, had a stake in Tim's case. After all, was he not a star patient of Mr. Blair Marston's, and was not the brilliant

7

young surgeon the most important consultant at St. Catherine's? Mr. Marston had been ready to stake his professional reputation on the operation which he had performed on the boy, in direct opposition to the opinion of several of his older colleagues, who had hesitated because of an unusual complication.

Those other doctors had told the child's father that he would never survive an operation; only Blair Marston had been ready to take the risk, certain that he could be successful.

Reaching up, Jean took the chart from its place at the head of the bed. She was still studying it intently when the curtains beside her parted again, and a man's deep, pleasant voice said:

"Good afternoon, Sister. Everything O.K.?"

"Good afternoon, Mr. Marston." As she rose, she would, if her mind had not forbidden it, have been seeking a reason for the odd tricks her heart played in these days. "Yes, everything seems to be in order."

"That's fine." Blair Marston's quick smile broke the gravity of his face, and as she moved round to the other side of the bed he took her place.

A little hand had crept out from under the bedclothes again, and was moving restlessly as though seeking something. The surgeon's sensitive fingers closed firmly about the thin wrist, and with his eyes on his watch he began to count the pulse beats.

Watching him Jean was disturbingly aware of the man whose grey-blue eyes could soften into such tenderness for a sick child. There was an air of quiet strength about Blair Marston which seemed to fill the small space of the cubicle: a sense of security which Jean was far from being the first person to find comforting.

While his attention was concentrated on the child in the bed, the memory of her first meeting with him was clear as a flash-back on a cinema screen. She seemed to see herself moving to meet the tall commanding figure in his white coat, a collection of students at his heels. She had heard about the "new man", whose name was fast becoming famous as one

8

of the cleverest of the younger surgeons of the day, and had wondered how they were destined to get on together. It was whispered that he could be a martinet, though he was also capable of kindness and consideration for those who worked under, or with him — if they were ready to go the way he expected them to.

Long since Jean had learnt how the firm, well cut, rather stern mouth could soften into gentleness and humour when he talked to his little patients, and she thought it seemed all wrong for a man like that to have no wife or child of his own. Those who knew him well said he was completely wedded to his work, and her own observation agreed with that opinion. Again and again through this last six months she had convinced herself it was the brilliant surgeon who interested her, and the fact of his being so often in her thoughts only natural, considering the part she was forced to play in his professional life. Even if he had been conscious of her existence apart from that, she knew that neither he nor any other man could ever mean anything to her.

The love that brought companionship; home; all the things a girl needs and longs for, was not for her. Any hope of it had been shut out of her life years ago, and she had dedicated herself to her chosen profession as completely as a nun to her vocation. She was certain that nothing would ever induce her to turn from that path, however lonely it might be.

In spite of all the good she was doing, it was a strangely bleak outlook for a girl still in her twenties; the kind of girl who had surely been made for a far less impersonal sort of dedication.

While she watched him, only half conscious she was doing so, Blair Marston looked up and their eyes met. She had become used to the intent way in which it was characteristic of him to regard anyone to whom he happened to be speaking, but now behind that grey-blue glance she saw a sudden warmth, a new awareness which made her breath catch. For what seemed treble the amount of seconds during which those eyes held hers, she found herself incapable of looking away, and it was Blair who, glancing back to the bed, broke

9

the frightening spell which seemed to have descended on her.

"I think all should go well, Sister," he said, releasing his patient's wrist and rising.

Aware of something that actually bordered on panic, at work in her, Jean agreed with deceptive composure:

"Yes, I see no reason why it should not. We will certainly do our utmost for him."

"I know that. I could not wish for a better team." He smiled. "We'll manage it between us. Another feather in the cap of 'Cinderella'. I wonder if you've kept count of the many successful cases we send out?"

"That's what we are here for." Thank heaven for the steadiness of her voice, while the din that growingly unmanageable heart was making seemed to fill the cubicle. But that there should be any echo of that clamour, in the breast of the man opposite her, was still far from her mind.

Marston said: "He has stood up to it all magnificently. I shall be in first thing in the morning. No need to tell you that the important thing is to keep him as quiet as possible for the next few days. Let him sleep as much as he can. The rest is up to his nurses."

Just then Nurse Summers came back, and after pausing to have a word with her the surgeon followed Jean out of the cubicle. He had done his round earlier, and only this very special case had brought him back to the ward again.

Walking beside Sister he asked abruptly: "When are you going on holiday?"

"Not for another three weeks," she replied.

"Good. By then Tim will be ready to convalesce. Mr. Barrington is taking him to his sister's house in Cornwall."

"He will be well looked after there?" Jean asked quickly.

"Oh, yes, his father will see to that. John Barrington is staying in England to be with him. He would have taken Tim to the South of France, but he's anxious for him to remain in closer touch with me. Though by then the boy should be well on the road to fitness, and I don't want him made an invalid of. This had been done to enable him to do all the things other little boys of his age do—within, of course, limitations, for a few months." That quick, charming smile broke the gravity of the handsome face. "Mr. Barrington's sister has three children of her own," he continued, "and a nanny who took a nursing degree before she decided to give it up for her present kind of job. Tim ought to be all right. You can bet his father will see that he is."

"He is devoted to the boy, isn't he?" Jean asked.

Blair nodded. "Yes. He would have given more than his fortune to buy his son health. I am glad to say that was not necessary." He stopped as they reached the entrance to the ward. "Poor little chap," he added, half to himself.

Unable to restrain the question, Jean asked: "Mr. Marston—the mother? Has she made no attempt to see him? Surely Mr. Barrington would have—"

"Allowed her to come? Not a doubt of it, if she had shown any sign of wanting to. The lady is, however, otherwise engaged."

"They are divorced? I wondered if, having got the custody of the boy, he had made difficulties?"

"Good heavens, no! Apparently Mrs. Barrington makes her son the last consideration in her life."

"That sounds—rather heartless."

"Yes. But I gather she is a born career woman. She's in America now. She should never have married." His voice hardened. Then, his expression changing: "The poor little chap has led a lonely life—not being strong enough to go to school and mix with other children. That was why I was so anxious to get him here, and why I put him in a ward like this, rather than in the private wing. As soon as he is well enough, he can be moved right into the ward, where he will be surrounded by other children and have the chance of making friends with them—" He broke off, and looking round Jean saw that the Staff Nurse had come up and was hovering in the background.

Dividing a smile between the consultant and Jean, Lorna Temple said: "I beg your pardon, Sister, but could I have just a word with you?"

"Yes. What is it? Excuse me, Mr. Marston—" Jean turned and they moved a few paces away. What Lorna wanted to say merely concerned a routine matter and could easily have waited. While she dealt with it Jean fully expected that Blair would have gone, but when she glanced back at the entrance he was still there.

With another smiling look in his direction Lorna was turning away when he moved forward, making a sign to her to stop.

"Hello, Lorna," he said, "I am sure Sister will forgive me for delivering a message I have for you." He glanced enquiringly at Jean.

"Certainly. Good afternoon, Mr. Marston." She turned away, leaving the other two together.

II

But walking away, she was curiously conscious of them — Lorna with the red-gold hair beneath her cap framing a face in which those usually sleepy green eyes seemed always to be provocative when there was a male about. Always generous to beauty in others, Jean was ready to admit that, however trying her Staff Nurse might be, she was undoubtedly a decorative young woman; though that did not excuse the way she was inclined to take advantage of the fact that she and the senior consultant were cousins.

But certainly she was an attractive piece; at least all the doctors seemed to find her so, and apparently she had a large collection of male admirers outside the hospital. That she, in turn, was more attracted to her cousin than the relationship excused was plain to all the ward staff. More than once Jean had heard comments, and snubbed the commentator ruthlessly. But — was Lorna really out to get him?

She dismissed the question abruptly. It was not the first time it had been in her mind, and it brought a stab of disturbance with it; for how could one help knowing that Lorna would not be the right wife for him! Again Jean tried to dismiss the thought abruptly. Blair Marston's private life was nothing to do with her . . .

Meanwhile Blair was saying: "It is only that my mother

sent her love and if you are free this week-end, Annette is going down there and there will be a party of sorts."

"Lovely!" Lorna exclaimed. "It's my free week-end. Tell Auntie I would adore to go."

"She also said that she tried to ring you—she was in London yesterday. She came up to do some shopping and went to the Haymarket with me in the evening. She was told you were out, when she rang before dinner, and you know her allergy for writing letters."

"I do indeed. Too bad. I was—dining out. I should have loved a word with her. I'll ring her," said Lorna. "Any hope of seeing you down there?"

"Afraid not. Be seeing you, though." He gave her a friendly nod. Then to her annoyance, instead of going on his way, he crossed over to where Jean was standing talking to one of the other nurses.

"Please forgive me, Sister," he apologised. "That was very unorthodox, but my mother asked me to deliver a message to my cousin, and I thought I had better seize the opportunity before I forgot! Which reminds me, I am off on Friday—to a conference in Edinburgh. I won't be back until Monday week, but I shall be in here as usual on Friday morning. There is just one other thing I wanted to say to you. That child who is coming in tomorrow—"

As they walked towards the entrance together, once again Lorna watched them, her slanting, long lashed eyes narrowing, a surge of jealousy and dislike flaring in her. The jealousy was for Blair, the dislike, which had been growing in intensity, for her superior. During these last weeks, if no one else had noticed the surgeon's marked friendliness towards Sister Campbell, Nurse Temple had certainly done so.

The deceitful so-and-so! she thought vindictively. *Playing up to him! Just as she played up to Matron, to get promotion over everyone else!*

That she herself had done a good deal of "playing up" to enable her to get just where she was, was of course, quite a different matter. Blair himself had helped, surprised but not displeased to discover his cousin's enthusiasm for nursing,

13

and little dreaming that if it had not given her opportunities for seeing more of him than would otherwise have been possible, Lorna would have owned long since that she had mistaken her vocation. Before coming to St. Catherine's she had been at a fashionable nursing home. It was only when she heard that Blair was taking up an appointment at St. Catherine's that the sudden urge to be in a big hospital where — as she told Matron — she felt she would be "of more *use*", had come to light. St. Catherine's was short staffed; a judicious word from a Big Man who admired the attractive nurse and had found her work in his patients (usually men) satisfactory, had helped a lot. Anyhow, here she was, and, fortunately for her plans, the complete inappropriateness of her presence in a children's hospital had passed by everyone except her fellow nurses.

Blair had always attracted her, and she was the type of young woman who, when she wanted anything, set out — no matter how devious the ways might be, to get it. There was nothing romantic about her feeling for her handsome cousin; she was the sort of modern girl who leaves "romance" out of a love affair, though she had had several in the course of her career. "Love" to her meant simply a strong physical attraction; but when she was married, other material things would have to be added. To be the wife of a successful, growingly famous surgeon, appealed to her. She saw herself pushing him on, entertaining lavishly, and finally becoming Lady Marston; for, with the right woman behind him, Blair was brilliant enough to go to the very top of his profession.

That he would get there without her help, or any ambitious desires of his own, was a consideration she ignored. A knighthood, or the more ambitious peerage which Lorna envisaged, was the last thing Mr. Marston would ever be likely to seek, caring as he did only for the great work which had always been the chief interest in his life.

And now Jean Campbell had appeared on the road along which Lorna had been so determined to travel to the goal she had set for herself. Even though he might be in ignorance of where he was going, Lorna saw that for the first time Blair was showing a more than impersonal interest in a girl—and that girl was not herself. It was characteristic of her to believe that Jean was deliberately setting her cap at him, and the fear that Sister Campbell would win all that she, Lorna, wanted, infuriated her.

It did not occur to her that Blair would want more and very different things to those she was capable of giving from the girl he married; or that, in any case, she was the last person in the world he was likely to think of in that way.

Chapter 2

I

During the next days no one on Cinderella had much leisure to think about personal problems.

Timothy Barrington's operation had been on Monday, and on the Thursday afternoon Jean was busy in her office — catching up on that conglomeration of paper-work which always made her sympathetically remember her predecessor's grumbles about all the red tape and form filling which, in these days, took up far too much time and left too little for what she — Sister O'Rourke — had rightly considered the more important parts of a nursing Sister's job; one of which was the training of the girls under her.

By often putting in hours of extra work Jean managed to balance things fairly evenly, but this week she seemed to have got badly behind, and so was using the afternoon hours in which officially she was off-duty, to catch up.

But somehow she found it difficult to concentrate, and even more difficult to rid herself of the depression which, just lately, too often gripped her.

As far as her work was concerned she knew that she should be very happy; only yesterday Matron had commented on the amount of cured patients who had gone out of Cinderella during the last month. Matron had taken a keen interest in "Campbell" since the day when the soft-voiced, dark-haired girl had come for her first interview and been so convinced of her desire to become a children's nurse. Her only reference had been from the Matron of a Northern hospital. Miss Stirling had written that Jean Campbell was a magnificent nurse, and that for her own part she would much rather keep than recommend her. She had added that the girl was practically alone in the world, and that her father had been the Minister in — Miss Stirling understood — some far Hebridean island, where her sole surviving relative still lived. She had nothing but good to say of the young nurse, and would add that she had been born to the profession she had chosen.

Jean's personality had tipped the scale in her favour, and Matron had certainly never had the smallest cause to regret her decision.

And now Sister Campbell was wondering whether it might not be wiser for her own peace of mind if she gave up all that she had worked so hard to attain; turned her back on the hospital she loved, and went somewhere abroad, where in hard work and a new dedication it might be possible to escape from something that was only going to bring her suffering — for heaven knew, she had had more than her share of that already. A little while ago she had actually begun to believe that the past was completely behind her, but suddenly once again a shadow threatened to darken her life.

The pen slipping from her fingers, she sat staring unseeingly down at the papers on her desk. Then with an impatient sigh she rose, and moving over to the window stood looking down into the courtyard below.

She had been there several minutes before a tap on the door made her turn towards it. When it opened in answer to her "Come in", Blair Marston paused on the threshold, asking:

"Am I disturbing you?"

"Not at all. Do come in." Hearing herself speak it was a relief to discover how normal her voice sounded.

He said, "I thought I would like a word with you before I go off tomorrow. I shall not be back until Monday."

"You will be away as long as that?" The words were out before she could stop herself.

He nodded, taking the chair she had drawn forward before reseating herself at her desk.

"Yes; I agreed to go some time since, and I can't get out of it. Let me see — your holiday won't start until after my return, will it?"

"If you are back on Monday, that will make it two weeks."

"Good. Will you be going to Scotland yourself?"

"Oh, no." The denial sounded more vehement than she had meant it to, and meeting the rather surprised enquiry of his glance she added quickly:

"I seldom go north now. There is—very little reason to."

"I see. But you are Scottish born—do forgive me if I sound inquisitive, but I have a particularly soft spot for that part of the world. After all, it's my Alma Mater—I studied for my degree in Edinburgh, and I've many friends up there."

Edinburgh! It was a swift fear that quickened her heart-beats now, not altogether banished when he added: "But that was nearly ten years ago. As a matter of fact, I am going to stay with my old Professor. He has asked me to lecture while I am up there—which I consider a great honour."

"They should be honoured to have you," she told him crisply, and feeling her colour rise was glad to have her back to the light.

He laughed. "Nonsense! I sneaked my degree and ran away. Then I went off to America for a year."

"But you came back to London." It was difficult not to meet his friendliness half way, and to her relief she was suddenly feeling more at ease. To have his friendship alone would be so infinitely worthwhile, surely she need not turn her back on that!

"Meanwhile," said Blair rather abruptly. "Young Tim Barrington progresses well. Friday should see him out of the wood. My colleague Maynard-Phillips will take over while I am away, and I don't anticipate any emergency."

In spite of Jean's determination to behave normally, the idea that for a whole week there would be none of those sudden appearances in the ward he was in the habit of making, and that she had grown to expect—in the way in which he had appeared on her threshold just now, brought the not to be denied knowledge of the blank there would be in Cinderella. She thought defensively that she was getting much too conservative where any change of routine was in question.

For the next ten minutes her whole attention was given to Mr. Marston's directions regarding what he wanted done during his absence.

Blair watched her, quite unconscious of the fact that he was doing so, or how at unexpected moments he would remember her face; the direct gaze of those sherry coloured eyes, the soft tones of her voice.

Looking up from the notes she was jotting down Jean met his intent look, and quickly lowered her eyes again. There was a brief pause, then he said abruptly:

"Do you get any time to yourself, Sister?"

She could not quite keep the surprise from her tone as she answered:

"Oh yes. And I have a week-end every month, you know."

He said: "I ask, because I was wondering if, when you have nothing better to do, you would come down into the country and meet my mother? She has a house not far from Colchester, and she has a particularly warm spot for the nursing profession. My sister was training at St. Patrick's when she met Robert Fairfax—who was a patient there. Apparently they fell for each other on sight! Anyway, she threw up all ideas of a career and married him. I know my mother would like to meet you, and I drive down there most week-ends."

Jean was conscious of an odd sensation, as though her heart had turned over—something which her scientific knowledge told her was impossible.

"That is very kind of you." Because of the rigid control she was keeping on her voice, the words sounded curiously stilted. "Thank you very much, but I'm afraid it would be quite impossible. You see, I have so many things to catch up with when I have a moment to myself—" She broke off, unhappily aware of how contrived and inadequate her excuse must sound.

"I see," said Blair quietly. That was all, but she felt as though a chilly wind had blown through the room—a wind that banged tight shut a door which, if she had only dared go through it, would have admitted her to something wonderful.

He rose. "Well, do your best to see that the hospital is still here when I return. And look after my patients."

"I will certainly do that," she replied. "Though as far as the hospital is concerned, I am only responsible for my own portion of it."

"I feel sure that will be safe. I shall be around as usual tomorrow morning — making a nuisance of myself. I must not take up more of your time now." Though he spoke lightly, she wondered unhappily if she had offended him. Then with a brief nod and a final "Au revoir", he turned towards the door, and went out without glancing back.

It seemed to Jean that she had never heard anything so definite as the soft click of that closing door. For a few moments she stood looking at it; then sitting down at her desk again she rested her elbows on its surface, dropping her face between her hands.

How unlikely he would be to guess the struggle it had been to repress her impulse to accept his invitation! she thought, conscious of that new stabbing pain that had no physical cause. That pain had lain dormant for some time; she had forced herself to ignore it, but now it was alive and not to be suppressed; the kind of heart condition even a brilliant specialist like Blair Marston could not cure. How ironic it seemed that he should be the cause of it. Just now he must have thought her refusal to go to his mother's house ungracious to the point of rudeness, little guessing the temptation it had held.

It would have been wonderful to meet him in such a different, more personal atmosphere —

Don't be crazy! she told herself. *Where have you been letting yourself go these last months?*

Along a road which could only lead to trouble; to fresh misery and heartache. Only a fool deliberately bought those things. Besides, it was not of herself she must think.

She remembered — would she ever forget — that moment beside Tim's bed when Blair had looked up into her eyes —

when she had seen that new awareness in his glance which had set her heart beating to a tune that however hard she tried to stifle it, would haunt her always.

II

While Blair walked towards the lift which would take him down to his room on the ground floor, there was a puzzled line between his strongly marked brows. He did not believe for a moment that Jean's refusal of his invitation to meet his relatives had been intended as a snub. But it was not the first time he had felt her suddenly draw that invisible cloak of reserve about herself; only, just now she had seemed — easier to get at, less professionally correct in her manner. And then she had shrunk behind that extraordinary barrier of reserve.

Why?

What was that reserve born of? Shyness? No, she could not be shy, she was far too used to meeting strangers, adapting herself to all sorts of people and conditions. But always, just as the barrier between them, which he had found it impossible not to be conscious of, seemed about to fall, she erected it again. And he had the same feeling which had come to him just now, of being shut out.

Did it matter? Without attempting to answer that question, he dismissed it from his mind when, a few moments later, he entered the room where the door bore his name in white letters against the dark surface. He had some notes to make before he left. Sitting down at his desk he scribbled them hastily; the typist who worked for him had gone home, and his secretary at his Wimpole Street rooms would also have packed up before he got back. It was already six o'clock, and he had visits to make to another hospital and a nursing home, in both of which he had patients whom he must see and give directions about before leaving London. That should finish his day's work — as much as it ever did finish. He never could be sure that an emergency would not crop up, to recall him either here or elsewhere. As well as his hospital appointments and his work for the big nursing home that was run for the famous trust of which he was a member of the committee, he had a considerable private practice, and though, as a consultant, he was not on call as he would have been in general practice, having taken his fee he did not consider he had done all that should be expected of him. It was what he expected of himself that mattered, and that was an unfailing vigilance to his cases.

Having finished writing, he checked the notes, and remained staring thoughtfully down at his desk.

But it was not that red leather surface, or the pad of paper he was seeing. Between those things and his intent gaze came the vision of a girl's face — cream skinned and golden eyed beneath the starched cap on her brown hair.

She was so marvellously *restful!*

Startled by the clearness of the memory, he rose quickly, pushing back his chair. Of course it was only natural for him to feel an interest in her, and for that interest to have deepened. Only natural to speculate about her private life?

He wondered suddenly if there might not be some very tangible reason for her apparent determination not to admit him into that life. She wore no ring, but there could easily be some man who was — important to her. The idea brought a curiously strong dissatisfaction. What kind of man would a girl like that choose? One never knew.

He hoped that unknown about whom he was pondering, with what she would probably consider unwarrantable impertinence! was the right kind — for her. Anyhow, at present she had been, and was being, of inestimable value to a very important case of his, and he was grateful.

But were those the only reasons for remembrance of her to be so sharply etched in his mind? And — to come so often back to him? . . .

Chapter 3

I

When Jean went back to her ward, to take a last look round, it was supper time for the small patients. In an hour the night staff would take over; Lorna Temple was superintending the two young nurses who were serving the meal, and when Jean passed her Staff Nurse said:

"Oh, Sister! Do you want Summers to remain in that cubicle the whole time? She seems to have decided she is a fixture there—"

Jean paused and turned back. "Someone must be with Tim." There was a sudden crispness to her tone. "Mr. Marston's orders are that he must not be left alone. Night Sister already knows that, and she has an extra nurse who will stay with him when Summers is off." It was more difficult than usual to repress the sense of irritation Temple roused in her. Surely she should remember how essential it was for the little boy not to be left alone.

Lorna gave an impatient half shrug. "Yet *we* are not supposed to have a special, though we are short staffed and rushed off our feet."

"As I told you before—six able-bodied young women can surely cope in the daytime," Jean told her, a cold edge to the words.

"Of course, we can *cope*," Lorna agreed, a hint of sulkiness in her manner. "It's just that we really have enough on our plates. With Robeson off sick, Summers is the only one I can really depend on to do as she is told—I told Blaker to get that bed made up, and she seemed to think the first year student should do it—"

"Try asking her nicely. She's quite easy to manage." A smile softened the asperity of Jean's tone.

"Good heavens! Where's discipline going to, if one's got to beg one's assistant to do as she is told!" exclaimed Lorna, flushed with annoyance.

That was not altogether unreasonable, but somehow Jean was not so willing to admit it as she might have been if she had not felt that it was Temple's manner, and not unwillingness on Blaker's part, that was responsible for friction.

"Anyway, I am going to sit with Tim for half an hour now," she said. "I will tell Summers to come and help." Going on her way she was both annoyed and worried. She believed strongly in running her ward on team spirit, and there had never been any trouble until Lorna joined the staff. There was no escaping the fact that Nurse Temple was a mischief maker. The Sister in the ward where she had been before she came to Cinderella made no secret of being glad to be rid of her; and she certainly had a way of turning a request into an order, and often assuming an authority which belonged only to Sister-in-Charge. Certainly, she was the last person who should talk about discipline, for it was not as though she ever showed willingness to be helpful herself; she had never been known to stay on duty a minute longer than the one in which she was supposed to go. She was, in fact, selfish to the core and never lost an opportunity of trying to get one or other of the younger nurses into trouble.

She watched Jean now, as the other girl walked quickly towards Tim Barrington's cubicle. Sister Campbell was certainly taking extra trouble over the Barrington kid! Any other nurse would have accepted that unquestioningly but Lorna suspected little Tim was getting extra special attention because Sister was anxious to please "Mr. Marston".

And of course he would be *so* pleased with her careful treatment of his star patient: the one on whom he had pulled off a thousand to one chance, against the advice of all his colleagues! There was a sudden vindictive light in those green eyes, as Lorna told herself that if Jean thought she was going to ingratiate herself with Blair to *that* extent, she would before long find she was very much mistaken! . . .

II

It had always seemed to Jean that the days were never really long enough to hold all the things that filled them. But during that next week, for the first time in her nursing career, time seemed to halt — even to hang heavily on her hands. On the Monday morning she woke with the feeling that something was wrong. She could not think what it was; or could it be that she shied away from the knowledge? But when the ward door opened at the usual time to admit the Consultant who had taken over for Blair, her reaction was one of almost outraged resentment that her domain should be invaded by this stranger.

Mr. Maynard-Phillips was an older man than Blair, a well known and highly efficient pediatrician, and a charming person into the bargain. He had attended small patients of his own in Cinderella several times, and Jean told herself it was ridiculous to resent having to adapt herself to his ways.

She must be getting into a rut, if she was becoming so conservative that she hated any sort of change! She really would have to snap out of it.

Mr. Maynard-Phillips was still in his early fifties, and extremely handsome, with a magnificent head of pure white hair, and vivid blue eyes.

With her inevitable reaction to any attractive male Lorna was all smiles, and obviously ready to be as co-operative as possible. Although she only had the rôle of second fiddle, she was determined to make a show of how tender and sweet she could be with the children, and in a subtle way she managed to make Blair's deputy decide that this good looking staff nurse was more "human" than the admittedly marvellously efficient but reserved Charge Sister.

When his round had finished on the first morning, and

the ward doors shut behind the handsome, suave figure and his students, Lorna exclaimed enthusiastically:

"That man's a charmer, isn't he?"

Sally Blaker, her assistant, who was uncompromisingly outspoken, shrugged. "He's certainly a bearable understudy, but I can't say I take to the idea of anyone in our Mr. Marston's place. There's a—kind of something missing."

"Honestly! Could one be more routine conscious!" exclaimed Lorna incredulously. "Blair would be the first to acknowledge that he was not altogether indispensable!"

Overhearing the exchange Jean frowned, wishing Nurse Temple would refrain from referring to the Chief Consultant by his first name. But she realised how that little argument had put a finger on what was wrong.

Until those wide doors swung open once again to admit Blair Marston's white coated figure, nothing would feel quite right, however normal things might be on the surface. After all, when one became as used to someone's ways as she was to Blair Marston's, having to switch, even temporarily, to someone else's, was bound to be—well, rather an upheaval.

There was another person in Cinderella who would most emphatically have agreed with her. Each morning Tim Barrington's first question was unvaryingly: "Will my Mr. Surgeon be coming back *soon*?"

Still their star case, Tim continued to progress rapidly towards convalescence. In spite of the attention and spoiling he got, the little boy remained a model patient—which was partly due to a naturally sweet disposition, and a pathetic gratitude for being given the feeling that people really cared about him. Being so delicate for years of his short life, and unable to meet other children on their own level had made him a lonely, dreamy little fellow. Now his strength was growing with every passing day, and Jean was relieved to note his anxiety to hasten the time when he would be moved into the general ward, and able to talk to the other children and get to know them.

His father came to see him every afternoon, loaded with toys and books, many of which Tim requested unselfishly should be given to "the illest little boys and girls". Not that John Barrington forgot those others. The millionaire was obviously regarded as a kind of perpetual Father Christmas, and appeared to enjoy the part.

Sally Blaker told Jean: "Mr. Barrington's not a bit my idea of a tycoon—except, of course, that he's obviously got oodles of money to spend!"

And Jean was able to agree that Tim's father was certainly not in the accepted image of the great company director of either fact or fiction. He was a slender man of medium height, grey haired and looking more like a scholar than "big business". At first Jean had found him disturbingly difficult to "get at", but now that they had become better acquainted she liked him a lot. She was sorry for him too; it seemed so ironic that someone who wielded such power over a great financial empire that stretched across the world, should have entirely failed to find success in his private life. Just as his wealth made unfailing news in this money-conscious age, it was more or less common knowledge that his marriage had been a tragic failure. His divorced wife was a well known personality of the stage, films and television; and had—as Blair had said—now gone back to the kind of hectic career that meant everything to her.

In spite of the quietness of his manner, though, Jean, who had learnt to judge people very correctly, was not really deceived. Behind John Barrington's unobtrusive personality she sensed the power and drive which had made him what he was today.

Although since his son's illness he had managed to arrange most of his business commitments so that he could remain in England, he had told Jean that because of something which had arisen he would be obliged to fly to New York this week-end; and on the Friday he said *au revoir* to his son with the promise that he would be back "very soon".

"Be a good boy, son," he admonished. "One day, when I have to go away, I shall often be able to take you with me."

"Don't worry, Daddy," Tim told him. "I shall be fine. My Mr. Surgeon will be back on Monday – won't he?" He looked at Jean.

She nodded, passing a hand over the child's dark hair. "Yes—and soon you'll be in one of those beds out there—and then you'll be able to talk to those other boys and girls."

"Oh, it doesn't matter so much about the girls!" observed Tim. "I want to talk to the boys!"

"Now if I could know he'd always feel that way, I guess the future might be simpler!" John Barrington laughed. "You'll like the little girls all right, son!" Then while Jean walked down the ward with him: "Tim's certainly devoted to his 'Mr. Surgeon', Sister. I'll confess I have missed Blair Marston myself this week. Glad he's coming back. I am under a great obligation to him. In fact, to you all; it is still incredibly exciting to know my son is going to be able to live a normal life."

Jean said quietly, "Mr. Marston has done a magnificent piece of work."

"You're telling me. There is nothing *I* can do, that would ever be adequate repayment. I wish there was."

"Tim's health will repay him fully—I am quite sure of that," she told him.

"He's a fine person," the millionaire said enthusiastically. "But I don't suppose I need to point that out—you will have seen it proved many times."

"Yes," she agreed. But though she appeared her usual serene, unruffled self when she bade him goodbye, there was a little added colour in her cheeks, and there was a thoughtful expression in Barrington's eyes as he walked away.

Turning into her office Jean paused beside her desk, her eyes on the small gilded perpetual calender which stood on it. That gadget had been a present from a patient's grateful parent; today it told her that this was Friday the 20th of the month. There would be Saturday, Sunday, and then—Monday. Only two days before Blair would be back again!

Too conscious of what that knowledge brought to her she thought challengingly: *Of course I shall be glad to see him.*

But she must not let herself remember how blank the days

28

had been without him. She must be more careful than ever to keep their relationship impersonal.

How hard life could be. Must she not even accept this friendship?

Crazy to ask herself that question again, when already she knew the answer to it so well.

Chapter 4

But however determined she was to remain behind the
barrier of reserve which she had built around herself, after
Blair's return Jean soon discovered how difficult it was to
keep that barrier intact.

The rather deceptive quiet of the previous week suddenly
exploded into a rush which Blaker described as "a perfect
rash of emergencies!" There were two particularly important
operation cases, one of which now occupied the cubicle that
had been Tim's; then two badly hurt children were admitted.

The nurses were rushed off their feet, and Blair was caught
up in a backwash of things which had accumulated every-
where since his absence. When he made his round with his
students he had no time to do more than ask Sister the
necessary questions, and listen to her reports on her cases.
It was her job to see that the background against which he
worked was as efficient as it was possible to make it.

But in spite of everything the nursing staff still took it for
granted that Mr. Marston was always apt to "bob up"
again when he was least expected.

Tim, busy making friends with his fellow patients,
appreciated those sudden appearances of the surgeon more
than his nurses did.

And so another Friday came, and with it a rather blessed
lull which was all the more welcome, because Summers had
been posted to another ward — replaced by a strange first
year student; and another of the nurses was off duty with a
sprained wrist.

It really had been a trying week, and on Friday it was
five o'clock before Jean, who should have been off duty an
hour ago, turned into her office feeling that a cup of tea was
the most desirable thing she could think of. Even if she had

felt like joining her colleagues in the Sisters' Rest Room, the hour was well past; but there was still the blessed electric kettle in her office, and lately she had got used to making herself a cup of tea when it was possible to snatch the time.

She plugged the kettle in now. While she waited for it to boil, an unconscious sigh escaped her. It was unlike her to give way to fatigue, but just lately she had grown conscious of a sense of intense weariness which seemed more mental than physical. Was it that the courage with which she had forced herself to face life was running out? Of all things in the world she hated cowardice.

Am I becoming a coward? she wondered. A coward, because once again the future scared her! She was still so young, and suddenly the road ahead seemed to lead only to greater loneliness. While she could give her service, know that she was of some use in the world, life was bearable. When time forced her to give up her work—

She broke the train of thought abruptly. I'm getting morbid! she thought. It must be because she needed a break. After she had been away she would feel much better able to cope with things—

The kettle boiling dragged her from her unhappy reverie, and making the tea she gave herself a mental shake. The cup and saucer on the desk beside her, she was preparing to settle down to write her report when a brisk tap on the door made her look quickly in its direction.

"Come in."

"May I? Am I disturbing you?" Blair paused on the threshold.

Jean wondered what one could do with such an unmanageable heart as hers had become, but her tone and smile seemed perfectly normal.

"Of course. Come in, Mr. Marston." She rose. "You are just in time for a cup of tea—if you have time to drink it."

"That really is the nicest suggestion I have heard for a long time," said Blair.

"Then sit down, while I get it."

He sank into the chair opposite the one she had just vacated, and fetching another cup she filled it.

Taking it from her he said: "What a Good Samaritan you are. This is exactly what I want — though I haven't had time to realise it! This day has been just one darned thing after another. I did not even get time for a cup of coffee at lunch time — had to rush off to a committee meeting."

On the point of resuming her seat Jean straightened. "You don't mean that you didn't have *any* lunch?"

He laughed. "Don't sound so severe. Going without lunch doesn't bother me."

She had gone back to the corner cupboard, returning directly with an open tin and a knife. "Well, it ought to bother you," she told him bluntly. "I'd like to know just what you would say to a patient who came and confessed that they had eaten nothing between breakfast and supper. I'll guarantee that it would be something drastic! I'm afraid this is only a cake, but do please have some." Before he could protest she added hurriedly: "It was sent to me by — a friend who is a wonder at cake making."

"It looks delicious." He took a slice of the deep gold Madeira cake. "I haven't seen anything like that for years. I say," he added boyishly, "this is good!"

Jean could not help smiling back at him. But at the same time she felt an unhappy little pull at her heartstrings. Who had he to look after him? Of all men in the world a hard working doctor needed someone at home to minister to his needs.

There was silence. Unconsciously studying the handsome face opposite her she noted with a pang of dismay that he looked drawn and tired. There seemed to be no let-up these days, and she knew that like every other man in his profession, whether they were on the ground floor or the top, he was abominably overworked.

Then he looked up quickly, and as their eyes met the colour ran up into her cheeks. What on earth must he think of her — sitting there staring at him!

But Blair only gave her one of those quick, charming smiles that she remembered so often, and which always brought that quick little catch in her throat.

"I can take a safe bet where your friend lives, Sister," he said.

"Yes. That cake comes all the way from Scotland," she told him. "And of course it was home-made."

"I thought so. It's out of this world of synthetic muck that is fed us in these enlightened 'technological' days! We really ought to go into all that more thoroughly, instead of leaving it to the odd journalist to point out that we are being slowly poisoned. Artificial colouring that other countries ban; sweeteners that are almost certainly dangerous to health; 'edible' oils, ice cream made from heaven knows what — certainly not from the pure cream and eggs my mother's old housekeeper took as a matter of course."

"Get a royal commission in on any of it," said Jean, "and the answer is exactly — nothing done. Dear me, all this from a slice of Madeira cake! Do have another one."

"Rather." He paused, adding: "I don't fancy that any hospital food is exactly exciting."

She shook her head. "At least it's wholesome here. Kitchen Sister has strict standards."

It was on the tip of his tongue to suggest: "*Why not come out to dinner and find something more interesting?*" But remembering her formal refusal of an invitation he refrained, asking instead: "Is your friend in Edinburgh?"

"Oh, no — much farther north." Again he sensed that withdrawal, and accepting the cup she had refilled for him, said casually:

"I was only wondering if I could have done any commission for you when I was up there — without expecting an invitation to tea!"

She laughed, shaking her head. "I am sure she (she's a kind of adopted aunt), would be delighted to bake or cook for you. But she's far — far away."

"I see. Well, this is really super — as my young nephew says." Blair's quick intuition told him at once that she did not want to answer any more questions regarding the whereabouts of her friend, and he took care not to pursue the subject. He had often wondered about her background; whether she had relatives; what kind of environment she

33

came from, and what her life was, apart from the hospital. If she could have guessed how frequently she was in his thoughts, Jean would have been more sure than ever that she must not encourage his interest.

"Young Tim is doing famously," Blair said, filling the pause. "I could not have hoped for better results. Another week, and his father will be able to take him into the country."

"Oh!" Jean could not quite keep the dismay out of the exclamation.

He looked at her quickly. "You are going to miss him?"

"Yes, indeed I am," she acknowledged. "He's a dear little fellow." Her smile was apologetic. "I always set my face against any sign of favouritism in the ward. But —"

"The human element takes over!"

"Well — Tim's been rather an exceptional case. The poor little laddie is so starved for affection. Of course," she continued quickly, "I know his father adores him. But then Mr. Barrington is so often abroad, and he can't possibly whisk a little boy off to places that are thousands of miles away. Tim has told me that he stays a lot with an aunt in Hampshire, but reading between the lines, it seems that he must have felt rather out of things. Of course, he'll soon have to go to school now?"

Blair frowned. "Not immediately. Mrs. Chetwynd has three small boys who are as full of life as healthy youngsters can be. When Barrington consulted me Tim was staying with them, and I realised at once how little time those youngsters had for their delicate cousin who couldn't join in their games. He will go down there to convalesce, but this time his father will be with him — anyhow for a month." Blair frowned. "Frankly, I would rather Barrington had a place of his own to take the boy to; but he hasn't a home in England. He owns a villa near Monte Carlo, but that's too far away — I must see Tim again after he leaves here. Also, as I think I told you, Mrs. Chetwynd's kids have a nanny who is a fully trained S.R.N. and was in a children's ward before she gave it up to take her present job. She is an extremely capable woman."

34

From the way he spoke she knew he was not satisfied. After a moment's hesitation she said: "It seems so awful that his mother should not want to take care of him. I still can't understand how any woman could behave as she has done — not even a card all the time he has been ill!"

It was Blair's turn to hesitate. Then he made up his mind. "Bad etiquette," he said, "to talk about a patient's private affairs, but as a matter of fact Barrington told me that if you asked about his ex-wife I could hand on the information he gave me. It appears that at first he refused her a divorce because of this habit the courts have of handing any children over to the mother — even if she is the guilty party and quite unfit to be a good parent; there was no question of such an arrangement because Desirée Falcon (her professional name) refused to be bothered with Tim. So she most willingly agreed that she would let him have the boy and guaranteed not to attempt to see him — wait!" As an indignant exclamation broke from Jean: "She had never wanted a child, and she felt absolutely no responsibility towards him."

"It seems more and more incredible," said Jean.

"It is," he agreed. "But — Good Lord! I nearly forgot what I came to tell you. I have a case down in the country for whom I am anxious to get a bed as soon as possible. Any vacancies?"

"Yes," she replied. "The Danvers child is going for convalescence on Monday. Will that be soon enough?"

"Fine." For the next few minutes he was giving her an outline of the new case. Then on the point of opening the door he looked round again. "Aren't you going off next week?"

"On Saturday. I shall not be on duty after Friday. I am so glad Tim will also be leaving on Friday. I would not have liked to be away when he left. I'm afraid, poor wee laddie, he would have fretted."

"And you will be gone for — ?"

"A month."

"So long?"

"You see," she explained, "I had no break earlier in the year. As a rule we divide our leave into two portions, but we

35

were so busy in the spring that I told Matron I would wait until later; and now she very kindly insists on my taking extra time."

"Well, come back safely," he told her. "We shall talk again before you go."

The next moment the door had closed behind him, and Jean stood staring at the oaken panels before she went quietly back to her desk.

Duty—Duty! She bit back a sigh and picked up her pen once again.

Chapter 5

I

Tomorrow morning she would be off.

There would be a whole month in which to sort things out — either to regain a grip on her commonsense, or find the necessary courage to pull up her roots and begin again.

She had never lied to herself, but during these last days — since that afternoon when Blair Marston had drunk tea in her office — she had known that it was time to recognise how terribly important he had become to her.

It was cruel enough to know that in spite of all her care her heart had flown out of her keeping; but it was torture to realise, as every quickened intuition forced her to, that she only had to make one little sign of encouragement, and the perfect happiness of loving and being loved again would be hers. It was not conceit which told her that Blair was beginning to care for her — and more for his own sake than hers she told herself it must stop before it reached the stage where he could be really hurt.

Supposing she told him the truth? Heaven knew it was not the first time during this last week that she had asked herself the question.

The whole truth! So that he saw clearly — as of course he would — how impossible it would be for her ever to join her life with his; because the dark shadow which lay over that life might one day touch him and ruin everything.

Yesterday he had finally asked her to have dinner with him. He had said: "It will be my last chance of seeing you. I have to go out of town tomorrow morning. But there is something I want to talk to you about before I go."

In sheer panic she had told him that it was quite impossible.

She had seen that he was puzzled, perhaps a little angry at her manner. He had shrugged slightly and told her: "Oh, well, it will have to wait until you come back. Or—can I have your address?"

And she had answered: "I—really don't know where I shall be. You see—I am going to be moving about a lot—"

It was such a palpable lie that there was no wonder he had answered with a brief "O.K.", and walked away.

Thank heaven she had not seen him again. And how much better it was that he should be angry, that he should dislike her. Yet she could not understand herself. It was so unlike her not to be able to handle any situation in a reasonable way, but the very idea of hearing words which would have been the key to unbelievable happiness panicked her. She knew it was because she was terrified that she would not be able to hide the truth from him—that she loved him with all her heart and soul, but because of the shadow of her past, it would be better for her to be dead than join her life with his.

And today, to add to her unhappiness, she had bade Tim a final farewell. She had promised they would meet again, but—would they?

The little boy was really unhappy at leaving the hospital. Must life in future be nothing but partings?

She had been standing staring down at the half packed suitcase at her feet, trying to remember the things she needed to put in it, when a knock sounded on the door.

"Who's there?" she called sharply, and when the door opened a little way and Sally Blaker put her head round it: "What do you want, Nurse? I am busy—"

"Sorry, Sister," said Sally, obviously dashed. "But Proctor," (Proctor was the switchboard operator), "asked me to bring this along to you."

"Oh! Thank you." Jean took the folded paper.

"She said the caller said it was most important, so I said I'd try to find you."

"Thank you very much. I'm desperately packing, and trying to clear things up. I'm off on holiday in the morning."

"I know. Have a nice holiday." Blaker smiled and withdrew rather hurriedly, wondering what had got into Sister, who was usually so sweet.

When she had gone Jean looked down at the folded paper she held. Who could be telephoning her so urgently?

Then unfolding the paper she read the message.

"Will you please go at once to the Savoy Hotel and ask for Mr. Barrington. He will be there at eight-thirty, and wishes urgently to see you. He depends on you not to fail him and will be eternally grateful. The matter concerns Tim, and is very urgent."

What on earth! Jean read the message through twice. Why had John Barrington not asked her to ring him? Surely he could have explained over the telephone what he wanted?

However, it was obvious that something was wrong, though what it could be was a puzzle. She consulted her watch. It was after eight now.

With the instinct for punctuality which had been bred in her, she changed hurriedly into a street suit, and in less than ten minutes was hailing a taxi outside the hospital.

The cab was held up at every set of lights and it was after the half hour when she arrived at the hotel. Enquiry at the reception desk showed her at once that she was expected.

"Mr. Barrington, Miss? Would it be Sister Campbell?" the clerk asked.

"Yes, I am Sister Campbell."

A bellboy was summoned immediately, and told: "Take this lady up to Mr. John Barrington's suite."

A lift deposited Jean and her grey uniformed guide on the second floor where she was received by a young man, evidently some kind of secretary, who with obvious relief ushered her into a room where John Barrington, who had been pacing the floor with every sign of impatience, greeted her with:

"Ah, you have come! I was afraid you might not get my message. Come in, Sister; sit down. What will you have? A drink—some coffee?"

"Nothing, thank you." She realised she was seeing a

different John Barrington to the rather diffident philan-thropist-cum-devoted-"Daddy" she had grown to know in hospital. But her concern was for Tim.

"Tim?" she asked. "What is wrong? You knew Mr. Marston was out of town — "

"Yes, yes. I don't want Marston. I want you. You've got to help me out," he said.

"What can I do, Mr. Barrington?" she asked. "Please tell me quickly. Or shall I go to Tim?"

"No, he's O.K.," he replied quickly. "Sleeping soundly. The trouble is mine." And then without further preamble: "I want you to take charge of him for the next month!"

She stared at him blankly for a moment, then: "Did you remember that I am going on holiday tomorrow?"

"I did. That's my hope. Look," he spoke rapidly, "Just every darned thing that can go wrong, has. First I get a telephone call from Mexico calling me there to a business deal — you wouldn't understand anything about that, so I won't waste time. I must go, and when I get there, there's going to be a lot of untangling to do. Then an hour ago my sister telephoned to say one of her kids is down with measles — his school is closed with an epidemic of the thing, and Nanny will be nursing and what not. Now Tim hasn't had it, and I wouldn't dare risk him getting infected at this stage — "

"Certainly not!" Jean agreed.

'Well, what am I to do with him? Or rather — I want you to take the boy wherever you are going. I don't know what your arrangements are — *he* says you told him you were going to spend your vacation at a country cottage."

"Yes," said Jean. "A friend has lent me her cottage in Cornwall."

An artist friend of hers had offered to lend her her cottage while she herself was abroad, and Jean had accepted with the idea that she might spend only half her leave there, and perhaps the last fortnight in France. But lately she had rather regretted the arrangement. While the idea of being alone — of having an opportunity to think, to rest, and perhaps make some decision about the future appealed to her in one way, she had begun to dread the loneliness of an isolated cottage where there would be perhaps too much time for thought.

Yet this did not offer a partial solving of the problem which she could no longer avoid facing?

"You want me to take charge of Tim while you are away?" she asked.

"That's right. He's devoted to you, and frankly—how can I leave him to servants? Anyway, hotels are not places for a small boy. Now I've got it off my chest!" He smiled at her rather ruefully. "I realise it is a bit much to ask you to spend your hard earned holiday playing Nanny! But I really am in a jam. And you are the only person I would dare trust my boy to at this stage."

"Well, don't worry," Jean told him, serenely accepting the situation. "I'll look after him. But you will be back at the end of the month, will you not? As it happens," she explained, "I usually live outside the hospital—senior staff can—but *my* flat is in workmen's hands—something went wrong with the plumbing. It's only a tiny place though, and I couldn't leave Tim alone there during the day if—"

"It's all right," he assured. "I'll be back. I can't tell you how grateful I am to you."

"I think I am rather grateful," she admitted frankly. "I arranged for a solitary holiday, but—Tim will be marvellous company. We'll enjoy ourselves."

"Gosh, you're a wonderful person, Sister!" he exclaimed. "I never met anyone so dependable and unflappable. A million thanks. You'll collect him in the morning then?"

"Yes." She rose. "I can't stay now. I haven't packed yet." She held out her hand. "Don't worry about Tim."

And so it was arranged. The last thing she had thought of happening. In the taxi to which he had insisted on seeing her himself, Jean could not repress a smile. Poor millionaire! Suddenly finding himself in a position he couldn't cope with, and yet taking it for granted that he only had to say the right word to get things to go his way! John Barrington was a strange mixture. Tonight she had seen the side of him that, making instant decisions, must have helped build his vast empire. A lonely empire it must be, though; and the thing he valued more than all of it was to be once again in her hands.

Going back to his suite the subject of her thoughts was musing: There's a girl! Now if I were younger — less disillusioned —

Suddenly he wondered what Blair Marston thought of the girl who made things so much easier than they could have been for him.

Now if I were Blair — ! he thought; and left the speculation unfinished.

II

Jean put down the book she had been reading, and glanced up at the clock which stood on the mantelpiece in the sunny sitting-room.

Quarter past four. Rising and going through to the red-tiled kitchen she lit the stove under the kettle that was already filled, before going out through the open back door. A small kitchen garden climbed gently towards a coppice beyond, where she knew Timothy would be playing.

"Come along, Tim," she called. "Tea time."

"O.K., I'll be there in two minutes!" he replied.

She turned back, smiling. After a week she knew what Tim's two minutes meant — they would certainly stretch until the kettle had boiled. But he was an obedient child, and the impression of how remarkably unspoilt, which her experience with him in hospital had given her, had been strengthened since she accepted the whole charge of him. She had no cause to regret the responsibility which had been thrust upon her. She knew she would have been very lonely without her small charge, for her friend's cottage was even more isolated than she expected. The tiny hamlet consisting of one shop and a few scattered cottages, was a good six miles from the nearest town, but lonely though it was Jean had never felt at all nervous; and her young charge was the best of company during the daytime.

At first she had been very concerned because there were no children for him to play with, but like many only children, especially imaginative ones, he found plenty of things to keep him amused.

Perhaps it was because Tim had been part of her work there, that she found it more difficult than on former holidays to detach herself from the hospital—anyway, she was constantly assuring herself that must be the reason why what was happening at St. Catherine's in her absence was so continuously in her thoughts. She wondered if, when she went back, she would find that Blair Marston was on holiday. She had never enquired when he intended to go, but she remembered that it had been somewhere around this time last year.

Now that there were so many miles between them, it was somehow becoming less disturbing to think of him; and though she had come away determined to face her problems and arrive at a firm decision about the future, in these long, peaceful summer days problems seemed to recede, and she found herself shying away from the need to take the decision she dreaded.

But Blair or "My Mr. Surgeon" as Tim still insisted on calling him—would have been difficult to forget, for he was still her small companion's hero, and Tim was continually talking about him. He had told her seriously that when he grew up he was going to be a doctor too, "and cure people of *everything*" that made them ill!

She had prepared the tea tray and carried it out to a table under a tree shading the small lawn at one side of the cottage, when Tim finally made his appearance.

Running up to her he informed: "I washed my hands in the brook, Jean. Look, they're quite clean."

"You must have made the brook very dirty!" she said, examining the still slightly grubby little hands. "It will probably have to be disinfected!"

"Oh, no!" Then seeing her eyes were laughing he told her reproachfully: "You're teasing. Of course the dirt will run away."

She shook her head. "I'll let you get away with it this

43

time, but *soap* and water for the future, young man. Come on — there are sardine sandwiches."

"Oh super! I'm starvationed!" Tim, who loved long words and had his own ideas regarding them, but loved her sandwiches better, sat down and began to tuck in with the kind of healthy appetite it warmed her heart to see. "I could eat the cottage up — and you too!" he informed her between mouthfuls.

"There's plenty on the table without that, sweetheart." Filling their cups she was conscious of the very satisfactory picture he made. It hardly seemed possible that he was the same delicate little chap who had come into her care, and had been so near to relinquishing his frail hold on life — such a short time ago.

When the edge of his hunger had been taken off, Tim said suddenly: "I say, Jean — " She had told him since they came out here that he might stop calling her "Sister" and use her Christian name — "I've been thinking," he continued with grave importance, "and I want your advice. Do you think that if I wrote to my Mr. Surgeon and asked him to come and see us, he would come?"

Always he was back to Blair; and always that traitor heart of hers hurried its beats at the sound of the name. How mad to try to persuade herself that her problem had grown less important.

"Oh, no, Tim," she said hastily. "Mr. Marston is much too busy to come all this way. Besides, he may be on holiday, darling; he — he might not get the letter."

Tim's face fell. "Do you mean he won't be there when we get back to London?"

"I don't — " she was beginning, when he interrupted: "There's a car, Jean. Is it Mr. Tregellan?"

Mr. Tregellan was the grocer who came once a week for orders.

"This isn't his day," said Jean. "It's probably just another motorist who has mistaken the road." The lane outside the cottage ended only in fields, but because there was no sign-post, drivers not used to the district often turned down it.

Expecting someone to appear at the gate and ask the way,

44

she glanced towards it, and, the sun in her eyes, was dimly conscious of the man who had stopped his long nosed, shining roadster, getting out and opening the gate. Then almost turning the table over, Tim rushed across the grass with a whoop of delight.

Jean rose to her feet, her breath catching, as the visitor to whose hand Tim was clinging came striding towards her.

"Hello, Sister! I suppose I am the last person you expected to see!" said Blair.

Chapter 6

I

For a moment Jean could only stare blankly up into his smiling face while she gave him her hand mechanically. Then feeling his fingers close on hers she found her voice again.

"Mr. Marston! I never was more surprised. But how — where — " she stopped.

"How did I find out where you were?" he asked. "Well first, John Barrington rang me from the airport before he left for Mexico, and told me how you had come to the rescue over young Tim. But he was in a frightful hurry and though he said you were bringing his son to Cornwall, he gave no further details. But when I arranged to stay with a friend who lives in this part of the world I thought there might be an opportunity to have a look at my young patient, so I got your address out of Matron. I ought to have seen him again before this."

Something she had forgotten.

"Of course." Realising that while he spoke he had still retained her hand Jean withdrew it. She had outwardly recovered her usual poise.

"So here I am," he added, "turning up like the proverbial bad penny."

"No! A lovely shining penny!" exclaimed Tim indignantly.

Joining in Blair's laughter made the situation more normal.

"You're just in time for some tea," Jean said. "I'll get another cup — "

"Please," he protested quickly. "If you have one here, I'd like it. Otherwise — not."

46

Reacting unconsciously to the authority of his tone she told Tim to go and fetch another cup and saucer. "And please, darling," she added, "be careful!"

The little boy ran off, giving a slightly anxious glance over his shoulder.

Seeing it Jean said: "I think he's afraid you might disappear. Do come and sit down."

Following her to the table Blair wondered how pleased — or otherwise — she was to see him, and if she guessed Tim was not his only reason for coming here.

He said easily: "I seem to have a habit of scrounging cups of tea from you. That young man is looking very well."

"Yes, isn't he? He will be in the seventh heaven now. You are his principal topic of conversation!"

"Good Lord, how boring!" He lowered himself into the chair opposite her, and then with a keen look: "What about you? Are you not having a rather more responsible holiday than you should? You needed a rest."

She coloured faintly, too conscious of a disturbing breathlessness. "I am enjoying it tremendously," she assured. "Tim is no trouble, and he's grand company."

"But you are rather tied, are you not?"

"Not more than I want to be. There's very little to do in this part of the world, you know," she replied. "I certainly wanted a rest, and I am getting it. A lovely holiday." Then aware of those steady eyes still regarding her she glanced away, knowing that his doctor's experience would find out things that could miss a layman's notice, and that in spite of the healthy tan she too had gained, there were shadows beneath her eyes, advertising too many wakeful nights. She did not want him to question her, and she told herself she wished he had not come. The next moment she knew how untrue that was, for just to see him again was marvellous — though heaven forbid he should ever guess how she had longed for a sight of him!

Returning at that moment with the extra cup and saucer, Tim asked eagerly: "Are you going to stay for the rest of your holiday, Mr. — Marston?"

47

"I'm not sure, old chap," Blair answered. "It depends on — circumstances."

"What kind of circumstances, please?"

Blair glanced at Jean, who was pouring out tea. "Just — circumstances!"

"But what are cir—" Tim began. Jean stopped him with:

"That will do, darling. Get on with your tea."

Unused to anything in the nature of a snub the small boy flushed, and Blair said quickly:

"Anyhow, I'm not going away at once. I'm staying at the hotel in Tregellis for at least a week."

"Oh, how super! Then you'll be able to come and have tea again!" Tim's spirits were quite restored.

"I'll certainly do that—if I'm asked." Blair smiled. "Better still, you come and have tea with me — or lunch? If Sister will bring you."

"I call her Jean now," Tim informed. "Mr. Marston had better, too—hadn't he, Jean, because you said it was holidays and not the hospital?"

Meeting Blair's amused eyes she flushed and laughed, then changing the subject tactfully, Blair explained that he had suddenly decided to take his vacation earlier than arranged, and was in this part of the world because he had been staying until yesterday with a physician friend who had a practice near Falmouth.

"How were things when you left London?" she asked. "At St. Catherine's I mean."

"Fairly quiet. My cases were all going well, and nothing exciting coming along. And as I discovered that Maynard-Phillips was going abroad and would not be able to take over for me later, I—came away. Your staff were running Cinderella quite adequately," he added. "Nothing to worry about."

"I didn't really think there would be," she told him. "Not being under the impression that anybody is indispensable."

He raised his brows. "Perhaps not *indispensable*. But you were certainly being missed." There was a dryness in his tone that made her look at him quickly, and as though in answer to the question in her eyes, he added: "I promise you there is nothing to worry about."

Jean longed to ask how Temple was doing. That she would be enjoying her brief authority went without saying; but Jean was afraid that the other nurses were unlikely to share her enjoyment. Though even if Lorna had not been Blair's cousin she would not have dreamt of discussing her with him.

Nevertheless, she could not stop herself wondering if, in spite of his assurance, he had not been aware that everything on Cinderella was not quite right. She had learnt long ago that he could be disturbingly observant, and would be bound to have noticed if there was any kind of atmosphere around. But she did not doubt that his remark about things running "adequately" would be right — while he was around. Somehow she was certain Lorna would see that so far as routine was concerned, there were no hitches.

After a little hesitation she asked casually how Lorna was.

"Fine, so far as I know," Blair replied. "She has not quite as much free time as usual, but that won't hurt her."

Was he really as uninterested as he sounded, she wondered, and hastily dismissed the question.

After tea Timothy took his friend to show him his favourite parts of the garden, and insisted on Blair being introduced to a fat pony in a field at the back of the cottage, that belonged to a neighbouring farmer.

"I'm learning to ride him," he announced. "And I'm going to ask Daddy to buy me a pony."

"That's a good idea," Blair approved. "Let's see how you look on this one's back."

When Tim had shown off his horsemanship they returned to the cottage where Jean had remained, ostensibly to clear away the tea things, firmly refusing any help. It was soon Tim's bedtime, but this evening he showed signs of mutiny.

"Oh, no, Jean!" he protested. "Not yet —"

"I'm afraid so. It's later than usual, sweetheart," she told him.

"No — please —"

"Now, Tim!" warned Blair. "Doctor's orders. Bed! But

I'll tell you what — if Sister will allow it I'll wait and come up to say goodnight to you." He looked enquiringly at Jean.

"Of course," she agreed.

"And you'll come again tomorrow?" Tim demanded anxiously.

"That depends. But you'll be seeing me again all right. Off you go. As long as you get to bed early enough you'll be so big and strong by the time your father returns he'll think he's got a new son."

"I don't expect he'd like that," said Tim, who was a realist. "Sure you'll come and say goodnight?"

"Certain. Though this is my cue for exit." Blair looked at Jean half apologetically. "If you really don't mind, I'll smoke a pipe while I am waiting."

"Please do. Of course I don't mind," she replied. All the same, the thought of being alone with him when Tim was safely in bed was — foolishly disturbing.

When he was alone Blair paced up and down the lawn, pipe clenched between his teeth, that thoughtful line between his strongly marked brows.

Would it have been better to go? Had he been a fool to come? After all, Jean had never encouraged him to hope that she would have any desire to meet him away from the environment within which their acquaintance had been limited. And even today, though her manner was pleasant and friendly, he was conscious all the time of the reserve behind it. She had not showed him he was unwelcome, but surely it was only wishful thinking that had made him glimpse a sudden gladness following her surprise at his unexpected appearance.

Heaven knew he had told himself again and again since their last meeting, that in hoping to make her care for him he was only trying to snatch at a rainbow, but any attempt to forget her had been useless. She had been too often in his mind for him to be at peace when she was away from him.

Seeing her coming towards him again, he knocked out his pipe and went to meet her.

She said: "Will you go to Tim now. The room at the top of the stairs."

"Right." On the threshold of the cottage he paused. "You must be cursing me for upsetting your routine."

"Of course not. Tim is naturally excited at seeing you again; you are the person who has made it possible for him to do all the things he has always longed to do, like riding that pony, and — But do go up or I shall have him out of bed again, bless him! There will be a glass of sherry when you come down, if you care for it," she added.

"That sounds good." He took the stairs two at a time, his spirits lifting.

II

And refusing to lie to herself Jean knew that for the first time since she had seen Blair last, she was as near happiness as she could ever be. This might be the only hour in which she would dare to lower the barrier between them — just a little. Let her remember every precious moment of it.

She had arranged the sherry decanter and glasses on a tray and put them on a table in the window recess when he came back.

"This is very nice of you." Taking the glass she handed him, he lowered himself into the armchair she indicated. "Aren't you lonely here in the evenings, or do you find plenty to do?"

"I read a lot. I brought some books with me, and I collect others when we go into Tregellis. Mr. Veryan — the owner of the pony — who has a farm a couple of miles away, gives us a lift when he goes to town on market days. There have been two market days since we came."

Blair wondered suddenly what the farmer was like and took an unreasonable prejudice against him. It was immediately dispelled, though, by Jean continuing: "He's an old dear. Very disappointed his grandchildren are not staying with him at the moment, because they would have been company for Tim."

"And is there a Mrs. Veryan?" Blair asked.

"Oh, yes. She's a sweetie. She walked over here yesterday with a basket packed with good things."

"Fine," he approved. "Pity the farm isn't nearer. This place really does seem isolated. I hope you lock yourself in securely—Abominable, isn't it," he added quickly. "There was a time when one would not have thought of anything unpleasant in a spot like this."

"Oh, there are no tramps or anything of that sort round here," she assured. "I'm not nervous."

"Of course not, but—"

"We're right away from the main road, you know," she pointed out.

But he would still have preferred the cottage to have been in a less isolated position. He said, changing the subject:

"The hospital must seem a thousand miles away."

"It does sometimes," she admitted. But she only allowed herself to realise now how much too far away it had seemed in those evenings when it had not been as easy to control her thoughts as she wanted it to be. How often she had wondered what he was doing—where, and with whom he was at that particular moment. And now he was here—and that stupid heart of hers was singing a forbidden tune.

Holding up his glass to the light and thinking that the deep amber liquid in it was like the colour of his companion's eyes, he told her:

"I'll confess that there were moments when I envied my friend his peaceful country practice with—though he works so hard—time for a life of his own, with his wife and two infants."

She shook her head smilingly. "I can't see you in a country practice."

"No? Well, perhaps not. Yet I seem to be eternally in a rush—chasing my tail and getting nowhere in particular."

"Except to the top," she reminded him.

There was a pause, then: "The top can be mighty lonely," he said, and putting down his glass, bent towards her. "It was because I was so lonely, Jean, that I came here today."

As their eyes met and she saw again that warmth in his which she had tried to shut her mind against so often, a shaft of fear shot through her. She knew now that she should not

52

have let him wait; she should have shown that she wanted him to go. To be here alone with him was the height of folly when — She broke the thought, saying almost defiantly:

"You came to see Tim."

"Tim was a very good excuse." He rose, and almost unconsciously she too got to her feet. There had been, she realised afterwards, some wild idea of escape — from herself, from the thing she had been holding at bay all these last months. But the window was behind her, and Blair, between herself and the door, blocked the way.

"Jean, do you dislike me?" he asked.

"No." The denial seemed torn from her, and with a determined effort — a last grasp at sanity — she forced herself to say calmly: "Why on earth should you ask such a question? You have always been kind, and — wonderful to work with — "

He stopped her with a gesture. "Yet you have avoided me as much as possible — forced me to accept that you do not wish to be friends with me. Was that because you knew it was not just friendship I wanted?" He was beside her now and had caught her hands before she could prevent him. "I never knew what loneliness meant until I met you — No!" As she tried to free herself. "Unless you are near, the world is empty. Listen to me and then send me away if you must, but believe that unless I can share it with you, my life will never be complete. Jean, don't you understand? You are coming between me and my work, my mind is obsessed with you. I love you — I want you more than I ever believed it possible to want any woman. All of you, my darling — all of you — "

Could one's heart sing both a dirge and a paean of joy at the same moment? She dared not look at him.

"Let me go — please let me go," she said.

"Not until you have told me — can you care for me? Will you — ?"

As he drew her closer she looked up blindly. Then she was in his arms, and with the flame of his kiss on her lips, knew that however brave the fight she had put up might have been, she was beaten.

"My darling." Blair's voice with that new shaken note in it reached her above the wild beating of her heart which seemed to fill the whole room. "I love — *love* you — I need you so terribly."

With his mouth against hers it was fatally easy to forget everything save his nearness, and the wild sweet tumult of her senses; to live only for these enchanted moments. So easy to give her lips where her heart had already been given.

When that long kiss ended Blair drew back a little, searching her face. "My dearest — do you care? Tell me you do — "

Her hands against his breast, feeling the throbbing of his heart beneath them, she tried to thrust him away.

"Please — please let me go," she implored. "Blair, this is madness. You don't understand. I must not listen to you — I dare not."

He took her face between his hands. "Look at me," he commanded. "Tell me that you don't love me — that I must go away."

If only she could find the words that would not come.

"Heart of mine," he drew her closer, "did your lips lie to me — just now?"

"You don't understand." A sob strangled the words. "Oh, if you love me, let me go — for your own sake!"

"Not until you tell me you don't love me!"

That was what she must do! she thought desperately. But though she forced herself to remain stiff and unresponsive in his clasp the denial still refused to come.

"You *don't* understand," she said helplessly. "Let me go and I will — try to tell you. I must not let you love me. And when you know why, you will know I am right."

Seeing the white agony of her face he released her. Then drawing her down to sit beside him on the settee he said almost sternly: "Are you trying to tell me that you are not free? Is there someone — You are not married?"

"No, no!" she protested. "But — Blair, I must send you away. You would know that I — dare not let you — " her voice failed, and studying her downbent face, he asked with almost brutal directness:

"Do you mean that because of something that happened

54

before we met, you are determined to sacrifice us both? What kind of man do you think I am, what do you imagine my love is worth if I could be ready to change, or thought you cared enough for someone else to—"

"Blair, it isn't that!" she cried. "I never loved any man until I met you. There has never been anyone in my life."

It was out, and knowing it was beyond recall she was suddenly aware of a strange sense of relief.

"My dearest! As if anything else in the world mattered—" He would have drawn her close again, but she pulled back from him.

"Don't! Be kind—I can't be strong in your arms, I— Blair, please believe that for your own sake you must let me go out of your life. After tonight we must not see each other again."

He took his arm from about her and his hands closed strongly on hers.

"What is all this? No, listen to me. Whatever has happened to you—I don't ask what, I don't want to know. Perhaps one day—when we have been married for years, if it will make you happier to tell me, I will listen. But whatever it was, it has nothing to do with either you or me. This is the beginning of *our* lives—nothing else matters. The past is finished with."

"Oh, Blair." Again there was agony in her voice. "Is the past ever finished with?"

"Yes. Only fools look over their shoulders. This is the beginning, Jean—our beginning." He rose, drawing her to her feet. As his arms closed about her again, her mind told her this was madness, things could not rest there. But even while her heart whispered that he was right, she was forced to remember what she had said to him, and to herself so much oftener—for his sake she must not listen.

And yet she was listening, and with his lips on hers the temptation to take just this little interlude of happiness was overwhelmingly strong. And Blair—had he not the right to happiness too?

That girl she had once been; the girl who had suffered so undeservedly had died, and another had taken her place.

55

She was Jean Campbell, who had earned a place for herself in the world, and the right to be happy. What had she ever done to forfeit that right? If she sent Blair away now she knew he would be bitterly hurt, he would have the loneliness she had once known. Even if he was unhappy with her for a little while, if when she brought herself to tell him her story — as she knew she must, whatever he said — he realised they should part, they would have at least glimpsed their Eden.

All these years she had convinced herself that because of the shadow on her life, she would never dare risk it falling on anyone else. For a time she had felt she hated men — with their greed, and their treachery, and their cruelty. But then she had worked with men whose ideal of service to suffering humanity had made her proud of their friendship. And she had been sure that her heart was shut away from everything but the work, and the children she loved.

Then Blair had come into her life, and from the first moment of their meeting, however strenuously she had tried to deny it, she had known that the capacity for the kind of love which she had believed quite dead in her, had only been lying in a frozen sleep, ready to awake at the right touch. She had known that she must not take his love.

And now — ?

Surely she had a right to her little hour, to take today and hold it fast, forgetting tomorrow. Again it was her heart that told her: *He wants my love. He needs me.* And as his arms closed about her she knew how desperately she needed him.

After a little while Blair told her: "I have another twelve days before I need go back. Will you do what I ask you to?"

She hesitated. "What is it?"

"I've chosen a cautious young woman, have I not?" he asked humorously.

She shook her head. "I'm afraid not. It's only —" but she left the sentence unfinished. It was so hard to explain.

He said: "Well, first I want you to write to Matron and tell her you won't be going back —"

"Oh, but I couldn't possibly do that!" exclaimed Jean and hurried on: "You see, she will have to find someone to take my place. And I don't think she would think Lorna Temple—"

"Lorna made a Sister?" he interrupted. "Heaven forbid! She's quite a capable nurse, but she is certainly not fit for authority."

Jean frowned thoughtfully. "That is the difficulty. You see, it will need some sorting out."

"Quite. A new Sister will be needed."

"To run your ward!" she reminded.

"Clever young woman! O.K.!" he laughed. "I am ready to compromise. You can go back until Matron makes her arrangements. But I shall tell her that I am not going to wait long. The sooner we are married, my sweet, the better."

Her breath caught. She knew she ought to point out that she had not promised to marry him, but all she said was: "We—haven't got round to that yet."

"But you are going to marry me, Jean?" he demanded.

A hand on his shoulder she looked up pleadingly. "Let us have these days without thinking or planning ahead. Let's make our plans when we are both back in harness." Hearing herself, a sudden fear gripped her. Already she was playing for time. How long could that go on for?

Chapter 7

I

If she was mad, at least this lovely interlude was hers — and Blair's.

Looking at her reflection in the dressing table mirror Jean realised how magically, during this last week, the years seemed to have dropped away. She had believed that she would never feel really *young* again, but now it was as though a burden had fallen from her shoulders and she was moving in a world that had been made only to contain her newly found love.

Blair no longer asked: *Will you marry me?* He said with supreme confidence: *When you marry me.* And however wrong it might be, while these blue and golden days lasted she was content to leave it at that; though it had taken a little argument to make Blair agree to postponing the announcement of their engagement, and he was insisting that she should tell Matron as soon as they returned to London.

Of course she still knew deep down in her, that there must be a very stringent reassessment before she dared to join her life to that of the man she loved, but she kept the knowledge tucked firmly away — determined now to live only for each day as it came. After all, whatever happened in the future, surely they would both be able to remember that for a little while they had kept the shadow of parting at bay.

Today was Tim's birthday, and Blair was taking Jean and her small charge into the town to do some shopping, and have lunch at the picturesque old inn overlooking the Market Square. While she pulled on her hat she heard the boy's excited voice calling: "He's here! Hurry up, Jean."

"I'm coming." She snatched up her bag and gloves, and

reached the bottom of the stairs as Blair's car stopped outside the garden gate. Tim was already there, and as he rushed to greet his idol, Jean paused involuntarily, her breath catching. Just for an instant a frightened question flashed across her mind. *Can one be too happy?* But it faded as Blair called gaily:

"Good morning. I hope you are in a birthday mood?"

She laughed back at him, and turning to lock the front door, said to Tim: "Have you got everything, darling? Your coat — in case the weather changes — "

"It won't change. It's going to be sunny all the time," he replied confidently.

"Of course it is. All day — and every day." His fingers closing on Jean's, Blair's eyes gave the caress the child's presence forbade them, for they had not let Tim into their secret; he had no idea of the real state of affairs.

As it was his day today he was to sit beside the driver.

"Now don't chatter," Jean warned. "Mr. Marston has to think about his driving."

Blair glanced round, raising his brows in that way which always made her heart feel as though it had turned over. "Not always easy!" he observed.

She coloured. "Well, anyhow it won't hurt that young man to keep silent for once!"

Nevertheless a good deal of conversation seemed to take place between the occupants of the front seat, until approaching the built-up area Blair was really obliged to tell Tim to postpone his discussion about what he would do when he was a doctor — which apparently included a partnership with Blair — "Because when you get old you'll be glad of someone to help you."

Tregellis was a picturesque old market town with a long winding hilly high street which led upwards into the square and down to the sea. But today was not market day, and in spite of a lot of visitors and their inevitable cars, the traffic was not too heavy.

So that when Tim announced that he and his "Mr. Surgeon", as he still called Blair, were going to get their hair cut, Blair suggested that Jean should take the car along and collect some household shopping which she had ordered the day before, she agreed at once to the arrangement, and having left them at the local barber's in a narrow street on the far side of the square, she took the wheel and drove off to do her errands.

Although she had to visit a farm on the outskirts, she was through sooner than she had expected to be. But as waiting was forbidden in the street where the barber's was situated she drove round the Square and stopped outside a tobacconist's opposite the hotel, for the car park was already packed.

The others could not fail to see her when they arrived, and she was sitting watching the passers-by, and the traffic, which seemed suddenly to have increased, when a man came out of the tobacconist's and paused to light a cigarette.

If she had passed him in the street she would probably not have noticed him at all, but now he somehow arrested her attention. He was a tallish man with a figure which she instinctively felt should have been good, but was running fast to seed; his suit gave the same impression. It was well cut and had obviously been made by an expensive tailor; there was nothing of the countryman about it. Both suit and wearer gave the impression of having seen better days. But it was not the rather bloated, blunt featured face that held her attention so much as the trembling hands with which he was endeavouring to light his cigarette.

An alcoholic! Her experience did not need to take in the mottled skin and the coarsening with which drink writes its tragic story. Watching, she felt suddenly there was something vaguely familiar about the stranger. She wondered where she had seen him before.

Certainly she had come across many of the type in the hospital where she had trained, and once nursed in one of the men's wards for some weeks.

Then he looked up and before she could glance away their eyes met. His — blue but faded now to an almost indefinite tint and with bloodshot, yellowing whites — were set rather prominently. He stared boldly, and for a moment she sustained the stare with a cold calmness she was far from feeling; for while she resented the inquisitive insolence of his expression, an odd little shaft of fear shot through her.

At that moment Tim and Blair, who had crossed the Square, came along, and running up to the car Tim called: "Jean! We couldn't make you look —"

And Blair said laughingly: "We've been trying to attract your attention. But obviously your interest was elsewhere —" He paused, adding rather sharply: "What is the matter?"

"Nothing. Why?"

The greying-haired, red-faced man was already walking away, taking with him that strange, unaccountable fear that had gripped her.

A chance likeness! She did not even know to whom, so why should her heart be beating so fast, and why should she feel the coldness which is said to accompany the presence of a ghost?

"You looked pale, that's all," Blair told her. "I wondered if you were feeling all right?"

"Only rather hot." It was almost true, the little shiver in her spine had left her. Now Blair was here that experience meant very little; yet she was subconsciously wondering if that could not happen again; if the disquiet which had not been with her for years, was going to return; the turn of a head, perhaps a note in a strange voice, the way someone walked or looked. Those things could give the impression that she had heard or seen them before — and because she could not remember why, fear stirred.

But thank heaven that particular man was no longer in sight, and the air seemed curiously fresher without him.

Ten minutes later she was entering the hotel dining-room, Blair ahead of her, to be greeted deferentially by the head waiter. And for the rest of the day Jean forgot the man whose stare, half bold, half startled, had been so disturbing.

II

But in a small, not very reputable public house in a more squalid quarter of the town, the stranger with his greying hair and down at heel air, was sitting in the bar, growing more thoughtful with every one of the drinks he could so ill afford.

Up to a point drink quickened rather than dulled his mind, whatever harm it had otherwise done him; and with each whisky he remembered more clearly the lovely young woman who had been studying him in that thoughtful, almost clinical manner, when his stare had sent the colour from her face.

Now—where had they met? It was years since he had moved among the sort of people to whom she obviously belonged. A big car, a child, and a man who, in his unostentatious way, "reeked" of money!

Jean! He sat upright abruptly. It couldn't be. Lord! there were millions of Jeans where he came from. But— Good grief! he thought. It could be. And if it was—

It would be an idea to find out if they belonged in the neighbourhood. He had seen them go into The King's Head, and he had a pal—a fellow countryman—working in the garage there. He'd certainly see if Jock knew anything, and if he himself was not making a big mistake.

"Why, laddie, you could be on velvet!" he told himself...

III

On the afternoon following his birthday Tim was wandering rather disconsolately about the cottage garden, finding himself decidedly at a loose end, because Jean had gone off with Blair and left him in charge of the cheerful, buxom Mrs. Loveday who came in three times a week to clean and make herself generally useful.

Tim could hear her bustling about the back premises. If he went in to talk to her she would probably present him with something delectable to eat, and tell him to sit quiet and be a good boy. But the idea did not appeal to him at all, though tea would be late today as he wanted to wait until Jean got back—she had promised to return by five.

Up in his bedroom where he kept most of the contents of his birthday parcels, there were enough new toys and books to make half a dozen small boys happy for weeks; for though he was so many thousand miles away, John Barrington had taken care that his little son should have plenty of packages to open, and there were also Blair's and Jean's presents. Just now he had only one of his presents with him, his father's chief gift, a gold watch on a leather strap which he looked at every few minutes, for it told him every time that five o'clock was getting nearer, though it still seemed a long way off.

A whole hour!

This was the first time he had been left in Mrs Loveday's charge. He liked her very much. She was plump and good natured, but he had been surprised and a little hurt when Blair announced that he was taking Jean out to lunch, and as they had "a little bit of important business to do", they were going to leave him behind. But Tim was an unselfish child, and had the makings of a philosopher.

After all, he had told Jean rather wistfully, he couldn't expect Mr. Marston to take him out every day, and added, "I expect he wants to talk to you about the hospital."

It was rather lonely, though. Earlier he had left the new cricket bat Blair had given him, with his ball on the front lawn, and remembering them he went to retrieve them. But it was not much fun practising the way he had been shown, all by himself, with no one there to bowl; then just as he was beginning to enjoy himself, a harder swipe than usual sent the ball high up in the air in a direction in which he had certainly not meant it to go, and before he could do anything about it, it had sailed over the hedge and disappeared.

If it had not gone right into the field on the other side, it would be in the lane itself, but as he was alone, anywhere outside the garden was forbidden territory; he had promised Jean on his honour that he would never go outside the garden unless someone was with him.

He ran to the gate and peered through it, but he was not tall enough to look over the hedge, and so he did not see the man who was coming along the short narrow lane until the other, rounding the bend, came abreast with him.

Tim could be shy, but his silence as he stared at the

stranger was not all shyness. He had been warned repeatedly not to talk to people he did not know, and somehow a first glance told him that this was exactly the kind of person whose acquaintance he ought not to cultivate. He did not like the look of the red-faced, rather pop-eyed man in shabby tweeds who stopped and smiled at him, and he was about to turn and run into the house when the stranger spoke.

"Hello, laddie. Would you have lost anything?" The unexpectedly cultured voice was the kind Tim was used to. He hesitated, then:

"Oh, please," he said, "If you saw my ball—"

"This one?" The ball was produced from behind the man's back.

Tim held out an eager hand. "Thank you *very* much," he said. "That is kind of you."

The other laughed. "Perhaps it is. It nearly hit me on the nose!"

Tim was too polite to laugh, though when he looked at the nose he wondered if it could have been made any redder. "I am so sorry," he apologised gravely.

"That's all right, son." His new acquaintance leant an arm on the gate, looking down at him.

Secretly sure that if Mrs. Loveday came along she would not have approved at all, Tim was even more certain that Jean would have called him away at once. But he could not help feeling that as he had to handle the situation alone, it wouldn't be good manners to go now.

So for a moment the man and the small boy regarded each other in silence, then the former observed: "This is a very pretty place. Do you live here—but that's a silly question, of course you do."

"Well—not exactly," Tim explained. "A lady who paints pictures really lives here. She lent the cottage to Jean, and I came—" he broke off. "If you'll excuse me I think I ought to go in now."

"Oh, don't run away. Your—Auntie, is it? wouldn't mind you talking to me," the other assured.

Tim was not convinced about that, but he corrected. "I

64

don't expect she would. Only you see, she isn't staying here."

"But didn't I see you in the town on Tuesday with—perhaps it was Mummy and Dad. I thought how happy you all looked." Pulling out a packet of cigarettes the speaker lit one. Noticing—as Jean had done—that the hand cupping a match was unsteady, and remembering that when his father introduced him to strangers he often felt "trembly", Tim decided the poor man must be shy and proceeded to put him at his ease. Standing legs apart, he surveyed his visitor with candid eyes.

"That wasn't my Daddy," he informed. "That was Mr. Marston; he's a very great surgeon. He made me well and able to run about like other boys. Now I'm staying with Jean—she's not my Mummy either, she's Sister Campbell at the hospital."

"Good grief!" exclaimed the man. "You don't look as though you were ill enough to need a nurse!"

"I'm not. But I was. And Mr. Marston made me well, and Jean nursed me in St. Catherine's Hospital in London." In the next few moments, without a clue to the fact that he was being cleverly cross-examined, Tim had told the story of his illness, the reason why he was here, and who he was.

"That's very interesting." The man took his arm off the gate, straightening. "Well, laddie, I'm glad you're better. Now don't lose your ball again. Good thing I took the wrong turning, wasn't it?"

"Rather. Thank you again." At that moment, to Tim's relief, Mrs. Loveday called to him. "I'm afraid I *must* go," he said.

"Yes. Run along now. Bye-bye."

Watching the boy run towards the cottage and disappear, the man lit another cigarette, his expression thoughtful.

Jean Campbell, eh? Well, well! he thought; and went off whistling, as though he had not a care in the world.

Chapter 8

I

Although he had fully intended to tell Jean all about that meeting with the strange man, the whole thing was put out of Tim's mind by the fact that she and Blair arrived back much later than he had expected them, having encountered an accident on the way, which Blair had been obliged to stop and attend to. They had driven the injured man to the local hospital, and by the time they arrived at the cottage Tim was in a state of worry bordering on tears. Being allowed to sit up half an hour later than usual comforted him, plus the promise of a picnic next day.

Having tucked him up Jean went down to the evening meal which the capable Mrs. Loveday had prepared before she went. Calling to Blair that she would be with him in a few minutes, she went into the kitchen to see that everything was progressing satisfactorily, and having lit the stove under the vegetable saucepans, was preparing the prawn cocktails for the first course when Blair came along the passage and paused in the kitchen doorway.

For a few moments she was unaware of his presence, and watching her he thought with a thrill how inexpressibly dear she was to him.

Then as he moved forward she looked up with a start, exclaiming:

"Dearest, I didn't know you were there! I hoped you were relaxing after your busman's holiday! The last thing I expected when we started back was that you would have to patch up unfortunate motorists."

"Good thing we arrived when we did. The fellow was lucky not to get it worse — I suppose he was blinding along."

Blair shrugged impatiently. "What were you looking so serious about?"

"I was thinking of Tim," she replied. "Poor little chap, he was in a panic, though he tried to hide it after we arrived. Mrs. Loveday said she was sure he had made up his mind *we* must have had an accident."

"Well, he's O.K. now, isn't he? But he certainly clings to you."

"I know." She bit back a sigh. "He's going to miss having me around. I wonder what arrangements Mr. Barrington will make for him? Apparently he isn't too keen on staying with his aunt."

"Anyway, he'll have to go to school presently, you know." But though Blair was fond of Tim, he did not want to talk about him now. He had come right into the kitchen, and sitting on the edge of the big table he told her: "You look wonderfully domesticated, my Jean. Somehow I've never thought of you in the role of housewife."

She laughed. "I was brought up not to despise the domestic virtues, and I assure you I am quite a good cook."

"I bet you are. Not that I intend to make a household slave of you. And talking of households, we shall have to begin home-hunting as soon as you get back to London — my present quarters are much too small."

She was glad of an excuse to turn to the stove. During these last days she had deliberately shut her mind against the future; but now she was suddenly reminded that it would have to be faced, and was forced to ask herself again if it had been altogether wrong to let him believe everything could be the plain sailing he expected it to be.

Coming up behind her, Blair dropped a kiss on the back of her neck. "Darling, is this entirely the wrong place to tell you how much I love you?" he asked.

"It is — if you don't want your dinner to be spoiled." But it was difficult to sound practical, or to think of anything but the joy of being with him. Turning, she found herself in his arms.

"You know," he told her after a few enchanted moments, "I ought to *make* you marry me at once, before we go back."

"Blair!" Her breath caught, but she thrust him gently away. "It's — quite impossible."

"Why? A special licence, and it could be done very quietly. You needn't even tell Matron before she finds someone to take your place." And as she shook her head: "Very well, we won't argue about it this evening. But don't you understand," he urged, "I want to feel you really belong to me."

"I want to. But — the potatoes are boiling over!"

As she turned down the burner they were both able to laugh, but she could not quite ignore the little shaft of fear which this time refused to be entirely quieted.

It was a happy meal, though, and letting herself drift back into the wonderful content of the bond of companionship which made their love so much deeper, she determined to forget that there were still problems to be solved.

After dinner she and Blair sat together in the oak-beamed, white-walled sitting-room, and it seemed as though, with the silence of the summer night wrapping the cottage round, they were safely shut away in a world of their own.

Resting her head against his shoulder, Jean was so quiet that after a time he looked down searchingly, and as their eyes met, gave her a little shake.

"I thought you were asleep. What are you thinking of so deeply?"

"Only how heavenly this is, and — wishing it could last for ever."

"Darling heart! I'm trying not to count the few days that are left before I have to go back into the maelstrom," he told her. "I wish that I could at least have taken you with me. Which is abominably selfish, I'm afraid."

She sighed. "I can't cut Tim's time here short. I forgot to tell you, I had a letter from his father this morning — he says he will be back at the end of the month, and has made arrangements for Tim to be collected. There will be someone to meet him, and fly with him to the South of France where Mr. Barrington proposes to spend the rest of the year with him."

"That is a good way to arrange things," approved Blair, "If his mind is occupied with the journey, it will soften the blow of parting from you."

"Yes, I suppose so." But she did not feel very happy about it.

"And talking about forgetting things!" Blair put a hand into his pocket and brought out a small square packet. "This was waiting for me at The King's Head and I meant to give it to you on the way back, but after we had seen to the accident victim you were in such a hurry to return—and it's really what I took you to collect." He smiled into her questioning eyes, and seeing the insurance marks on the little parcel, she looked up quickly.

"Open it!" he said.

She undid the seals, and stripping off the paper disclosed a strong cardboard box. In the midst of a quantity of packing there was another much smaller box with the name of a famous jewellers on it.

"It seems to be a kind of Chinese puzzle," laughed Blair. "All that is just camouflage because the main enclosure is too small to come through the post."

Her heart beating quickly Jean opened the second box, disclosing a white leather ring case.

"Go on, open it!" teased Blair. "It won't bite."

At a touch the case flew open, disclosing a square sapphire hasped with diamonds and set in a half circlet of white gold. Flushing and then paling, Jean stared down at it.

He said: "If you prefer something different we can change it later. I had to send to London for it, and I could only give them a rough idea of what I wanted—"

"It's lovely!" But this time the eyes she lifted to his were frankly troubled; suddenly the dream in which she had been living was turned into stern reality, for if she wore Blair's ring it would mean the passing of a milestone from which it would be impossible to turn back. And yet—

"Here. Let me." Reaching out he took the ring from its velvet bed, and then lifted her left hand. The next moment the sapphire was gleaming on her betrothal finger.

"My darling heart," Blair said gently, "that's the first

fetter — a visible sign of the claim I stake in you. I shan't be really content until there is a plain band under it —"

"Oh, my dear, if you should ever regret!" The words were torn out before she could restrain them.

On his feet Blair drew her almost roughly up into his arms. "Regret — please God! — is not a word that can be used about you and me," he told her. "What regrets could I possibly have — unless I ever brought you unhappiness."

"But if I should bring *you* unhappiness." A hand on his shoulder, she searched his face. "My dearest, you wouldn't listen to me at the beginning, but before there is any question of our getting married —"

"The question is already settled," he interrupted. "*I* told you — we are beginning our lives and I forbid you to look back. Nothing can make any difference — do you hear? *Nothing.*"

Why not believe him? If she gave him the key of that Bluebeard's Chamber, would he not still insist that they must not part? With the troubling sweetness of his arms about her, his lips on hers, it was difficult to think beyond her longing for the happiness that could never come to her without him.

Later she would try to find the way that was best for him. But with his ring on her finger the temptation to continue to do as he commanded — to take no backward look — was too strong for her.

When their long kiss ended, she hid her face against him, a half sob escaping her.

"Jean, my love." He lifted her face gently. "You are not really unhappy?"

"I am — afraid," she told him simply.

"But there isn't a thing in the world for you to be afraid of!" he exclaimed. "Have I not told you — *while you love me and I love you, as long as we are together, nothing else can matter.*" He stressed the words almost sternly. "And listen, young woman!" Authority mingled with the tenderness of his tone: "No shilly-shallying! We are going to be married within the next month at the latest. I shall have the licence by the time you arrive. I suppose the whole hospital will want to be at our wedding, but they haven't a hope. Is it unfair to do you out of all the limelight, to want a quiet ceremony."

"No," she told him quickly. "It couldn't be too quiet."

The voice of temptation was deafening her to the warning of wisdom, demanding: Why should the past stretch out destroying hands to snatch their happiness? Who was going to associate Sister Jean Campbell with—that other unhappy wronged girl? The questions forcing themselves into her mind brought sudden comfort, and she ceased asking herself whether she dared go through with it. For surely she would be mad not to accept the fact that some kinder Fate had sent her this chance to begin her life all over again? With Blair's lips against hers, the world once again narrowed to the circle of his arms.

"Dear heart, it's getting late. I must go." He kissed her again, quickly and closely, then put her gently from him. "I'll be here tomorrow—about ten?"

"Yes. We mustn't do Tim out of his picnic. I hope it will be fine."

"Of course it will," he said confidently. "Good night, my sweet." For a moment he drew her close again, whispering: "Soon there won't be any more of these goodnights. I shall have you—always." Then releasing her he went quickly into the hall.

As Jean opened the front door for him, he told her: "Don't come out. I still dislike the idea of you and Tim being here on your own. Mind you lock up."

"Of course. There's not a thing to worry about," she answered confidently.

In spite of his admonition she waited in the porch until the gate clicked behind him, then shut the door, pushing the bolt on it home.

When she went back into the sitting-room the clock on the mantelpiece was striking eleven. Collecting the coffee tray she carried it into the kitchen. It was past the time when she usually went up to her room, and it had been a long day, but she felt wide awake.

Her former mood of uncertainty and disquiet had almost

gone—it seemed as though, in shutting the front door just now, she had shut out all doubt and fear.

Everything was going to be absolutely all right, she told herself, her heart lighter than it had been for years; things seemed to have changed, for the first time she allowed herself to look with confidence beyond the immediate moment, towards the future with the man who was her whole life.

"*As long as I love you, and you love me.*"

The echo of his voice came back to her, quickening her heartbeats. She was turning towards the light switch when she saw that Blair had left his driving gloves on the table, and at the same moment there was a knock on the front door.

Looking back afterwards she wondered why she had felt no warning; no glimmer of fear; been so certain that, having missed his gloves, Blair had come back for them.

The light was still burning in the hall, and going quickly out of the room she went across and unbolted the door. Almost as she opened it the man on the threshold walked in.

"There's no reason to be afraid," he said, smiling at her. "This is not a hold-up. I just want to renew an old acquaintance, Jeannie Stewart!"

Meeting those bloodshot, prominent eyes Jean's heart missed a beat. It needed no effort of memory to recognise her visitor as the man she had seen outside the tobacconist's shop in Tregellis on Tim's birthday, but now she knew in a flash why he had seemed vaguely familiar.

II

"Well? Are you not going to say 'How are you' to an old friend?" He held out his hand smilingly.

She knew this was a time to think clearly, but her mind was clouded by shock, and all she could say was:

"I—I think there is some mistake. My name is not Stewart." While she listened to herself, she knew she was saying the wrong thing.

Above those pouched, suddenly cynical eyes his rugged brows went up. "Is that so?" he asked. "Maybe you've changed it, Jeannie, but mine's the same — Neil McNairn. Remember? Or is it true that you're rejecting the friend who came to your rescue — it will be six years ago now?"

However hard she tried to ignore it, she could not smother the little stab of guilt his words and the reproachful tone in which they were spoken, brought to her. She flushed and paled, meeting his glance steadily. "Why have you come here?" she asked.

"That's a long story," he replied. "Won't you ask me in? Even if it's not Jeannie Stewart, but 'Sister Jean Campbell' of St. Catherine's Hospital in London, that I'm calling on!"

She knew that it was useless to deny him. She must handle this situation as best she could; above all she must find out how he came to have the knowledge his words betrayed.

"Yes, you had better come in," she told him, pointing to the sitting-room.

"I'll shut this door first." He suited the action to the words. "An open door might prove embarrassing if your friend came back. And it's because I didn't want to embarrass you that I am making my call at such an unorthodox hour . . . After you."

He stood aside, then followed her into the room, putting his hat on a chair as he passed; then he walked over to the hearthrug and turned to face her.

Half unconsciously she had seen how shabby the hat was; his tweed jacket had been patched on one elbow, yet, as she had noticed when she saw him in the town, his clothes were well cut and he wore them with an air. But looking at him she realised it could only have been a gleam of something resembling clairvoyance which had given her the fleeting impression she had seen him before. It added to her shock to realise how altered he was; how the handsome, perfectly groomed, professional man she once knew, had degenerated into this down-at-heel, coarsened creature with "wastrel" written large all over him. And even in the state of near panic which she was fighting back she felt a pang of regret. She so hated waste. This was surely all wrong!

Meeting her eyes he read something of what was in her

mind, and a dark flush stained his face. "You're thinking I'm changed," he said. "Ah, well, you've heard about 'time's revenges'. You're changed too, lassie. I didn't recognise you at once when I saw you in the town two days since — or maybe it would be more correct to say I couldn't believe it was my little friend Jeannie — only your beautiful amber eyes are still the same, though they're not swollen with tears as they were. It was those made me sure it was you!" He broke off, adding: "I must say, I admire your good sense."

"I don't understand —" she began.

"You are not going to try to convince me that we never met before?"

"What good will it do to make me remember — where and how we met?" she asked. "As you know so much about me already, surely you must realise that I — don't want to be reminded. Oh!" she exclaimed quickly. "I don't forget that I am under an obligation to you —"

He flushed again. "That's as maybe. *I* certainly wouldn't have said it, but if you feel that way it may help."

"Will you please tell me what you want?" she asked.

He smiled at her suddenly. He had once had a very attractive way of smiling, and though it was only a ghost of that old self-derision, it could still alter his features sufficiently to make her see again the man she had once known.

"What I want most at the moment is a drink," he said frankly. "If you'd offer me one — or even more! I'd be grateful. Knowing I was coming to see a lady I had the remaining grace to turn up sober, but I've a thirst I wouldn't sell for a million."

She went to the sideboard, returning with the sherry decanter and a fresh glass. "Help yourself, please. I have nothing else."

He filled the glass, glancing at her enquiringly. "Won't you — ?"

"No."

"Then would you sit down. I'm still too much of a gentleman to sit while a lady stands." There was a note of bitter irony behind the flippant tone.

74

She sat down, and he sank into an armchair, the decanter at his elbow, his glass in his hand.

"Here's to a friendly understanding!" He raised the glass, drained and refilled it. "It's a long time since we had a wee drink together, Jeannie. As you may notice, I've rather come down in the world since then."

That was too obvious. When she had known him in the past — that past which, heaven help her! she had almost persuaded herself was dead — he had been more than half way up the ladder of success, though she remembered that even then people who knew him well had prophesied that he would not stay the pace. He drank too much to be able to give his brilliant gifts a chance to do what they should have done for him.

"It is getting late," she reminded him.

"I'm afraid it is," he agreed. "And I'm keeping you out of your bed. But if you will listen, I'll tell you what the situation is." Then instead of proceeding he filled his glass again, and holding it up to the light thoughtfully examined the amber liquid. "Just the colour of your eyes — as I said just now." He gave another of those wry smiles. "Oh, yes, I've changed. Rather different, I'm afraid, from the Neil McNairn of the old Edinburgh days: that well known light of the Scottish Bar — being a trained nurse, it no doubt occurs to you that I am more often concerned with another kind of bar. But I'm still the man who — no *obligation* on your part mind — was able, very willingly, to go to the assistance of a girl named Jean Helen Stewart whom we — both knew, poor lass!"

"I had not forgotten," Jean said steadily. But how desperately she wished that she did not need to remember that if it had not been for the eloquence and brilliant pleading of the advocate who had defended Jean Stewart during a certain trial in the Court of Session of Scotland's capital, the verdict might have been very different to that one of "Non-proven" which had sent an innocent girl out into the world with her name still not cleared of the stigma upon it.

"See here, Jean," McNairn bent towards her. "I'm down

and out. It's only a temporary thing, but I need help to put me on my feet again. That's why I'm here. I thought perhaps that for 'auld time's sake', you'd give me a lift."

"You mean that you want money?"

"Well—yes."

"How much?" she asked bluntly.

He hesitated. He still liked to persuade himself that he was not quite lost to all sense of decency. But his need was urgent, and after all, didn't she owe him something? He had helped her at the time without asking a penny compensation. If she had money now—and if she had not much of her own, he was sure she could get it, for he had quickly noticed the ring on her finger, and he did not doubt who had put it there. From the enquiries he had made and his own observations, it was pretty clear she was going to marry a man who was not only rich, but whom he very much doubted would be likely to know the truth about her.

He said: "It's not the earth I've come to ask you for, but it would make all the difference in the world to me—just a couple of hundred pounds. Look, Jeannie, I've got to have it. Otherwise, it's curtains for me. As you can tell, I'm pretty desperate."

"But surely you must realise I am not well off," she protested. "I only have what I earn, and—"

"There's someone who would give you anything he thought you needed," he said, dropping all pretence at decency, for it was true that unless he got the money his situation would be drastic. Certain people with whom he had become involved would stop at nothing unless he could pay what he owed, and though he had little in the way of reputation to lose, he had no desire to end his days in some dark alley—a victim of the kind of violence his underworld acquaintances were more than capable of.

For a moment Jean had been too startled to speak, but recovering herself she told him: "You must understand, at once, that there is no one in the world—*no one*, whom I would ask for a penny."

This was the last thing she had ever dreamt would happen — that of all men this one would come back into her life and demand help from her. For she had no illusions; she knew that this was a *demand*. And if she refused to help him, what would he do? He had said that he was desperate, and she had to believe him.

Apart from her feeling that she was in his debt, she was suddenly filled with an overwhelming desire to get rid of him — above all, to prevent him ever coming into contact with Blair. And yet somehow she was sure that, however low he had fallen, this man would not stoop to actual blackmail — if he was sober. But if she did not get rid of him, if he claimed her acquaintance, what would Blair think?

Supposing Blair came back now and found him with her? Unlikely as that was, since he had not returned at once for his gloves, it strengthened her desire to see the back of her visitor at any cost.

"You must know," she said, "that until I return to London — in ten days' time, I could not possibly get hold of any sum as large as that."

"You couldn't borrow it until then?"

"No."

He said with a half apologetic laugh: "I'm not lying when I tell you I'm skint. Look, I expected to get some work when I came to these parts, but I've been let down, and — I owe the place where I'm staying, and one or two other things. If you could let me have something to be going on with? The odd fifty perhaps?"

She thought quickly. "I could let you have thirty."

"That would be fine," he agreed, visibly cheered. "When could I collect — the rest?"

"If you could tell me where I can get in touch with you —" Jean began.

"I'd rather come to you and collect it," he said quickly. "Not at the hospital —"

"No!" she exclaimed. But she did not want to give him her address. As a senior Sister she had been able to avoid living in the St. Catherine's hostel, but she did not want him coming to the flatlet she had in the building not far from her work.

"I can ring you, can't I?" McNairn asked. "No need to give me your number," he added casually. "I can find it in the book."

He could, of course, do just that, and it was plain he had already found out as much. She wondered again what he would have said if she had refused him outright. Would he have been as—almost humble as this? But wasn't she crazy to let him have all he asked for? Yet her desire to be rid of him was too strong to allow any hesitation. Nevertheless she said firmly: "You do understand that I am doing this as a return for—what you did for me. I couldn't go on helping you—"

"No, no. It's a once only. Believe me, if there was any other way—But I'm friendless." In spite of what he had said earlier he had drunk a good deal before he arrived, and now he was reaching the lachrymose stage; there were actual tears in his eyes as he poured out the last of the sherry.

She looked at him, sick with distaste, though at the same time an unwilling pity stirred in her. He was so terribly altered; with all the signs of the vice that was killing him stamped on his coarsened features—the wreck of the handsome, brilliant man she had known.

She rose, telling him: "If you will wait, I'll get that for you."

"O.K.," he agreed. "And as I've your word that you'll see me in London, I'll be away first thing in the morning." He was smiling, but when she had gone out of the room the smile faded, and he sat staring at the empty decanter while the contents of his glass remained untasted. Whatever his faults were, unless he was very drunk he never indulged in self-deception, and he faced the unbeautiful fact that there was a very ugly word for what he was doing tonight. For even if Jean felt that she was paying for the service he had once rendered her, this was still a form of blackmail. He had never thought he would fall as low as that, and his knowledge—from that ring on her betrothal finger—that she was engaged to marry a man who was well off enough to compensate for any loss of her savings, did not excuse the ugliness of his conduct.

But it was characteristic of him to ask of himself hopelessly: "*What else can I do?*"

III

Up in her bedroom Jean unlocked the drawer where she kept the ready money which she had drawn from the bank before she came away. She was glad that she had brought more than she was likely to need; shutting her mind to everything but the urgent desire to be rid of the man who had come like some evil shadow from the years behind her, she counted the notes.

Strangely, she felt little resentment against McNairn so far as she herself was concerned; but even while she faced the fact that his reappearance on the scene was going to make it imperative to completely reassess her relationship with Blair, she was bitterly angry that McNairn, with his brain and his chance of success, should have thrown the whole thing away and let himself sink to the level he had so plainly reached. She was incapable just then of thinking about her own future, still stunned by the shock of tonight's encounter.

Tim's room was opposite hers, and when she went out on to the landing again, to her dismay she saw him standing in the open doorway.

"Tim! What are you doing out of bed?" she demanded.

"I was going to get a drink," he explained. "There's no water in my room."

"Then go back quickly and I'll get you some." She shooed him into bed again, and going swiftly along to the bathroom, brought him a glass of water. "You must go to sleep at once," she said sternly. "Mr. Marston would be very cross if he knew you were awake so late."

He snuggled down. "Has he gone yet?"

"Yes, of course. Long ago."

The next question startled her. "Who knocked at the door?"

She hesitated. "No one."

"But I thought he'd come back. I heard you talking to someone," he insisted.

She forced a laugh. "You've been dreaming."

He gave her a sleepy grin. "Time you were in bed too."

"I shall be very soon." She kissed him, and tucking him in, went out shutting the door tightly; she hoped he would not notice that, because as a rule she left it a little open. But the one thing she did not want was for him to know of her visitor. He would be so likely to say something to Blair, and she could not tell him not to. As yet she had not begun to decide what explanation she would give when she herself was forced to tell Blair she could not marry him.

She found McNairn where she had left him, staring rather moodily into his empty glass. Then he looked up and their eyes met.

He rose a little unsteadily, "Hello! I was nearly asleep. I can't say I feel like a long walk. That pretty village I came through will be as far as I get this night. Do you know if the pub can give me a bed?"

She shook her head. "I doubt it — at this hour they will be closely shut up."

He glanced towards the clock. "Good grief! I had no idea it was so late as that. I must be on my way."

She held out the bundle of notes she had brought down. "Take these."

"Thank you." He thrust them into his inside pocket, fastening his jacket securely.

"Hadn't you better count it?" she asked. "I think there is thirty pounds there."

"No need. And there's no need to give you an I.O.U., since I can see no possibility of treating your help as a loan." His lips twisted wryly.

"I don't think of it that way, Mr. McNairn," she said quietly. "It is — a debt I owe." She hesitated, then continued, unable to repress the impulse: "It would make me —" But she could not say "happier", and hurried on: "I would like to think it would help you to — begin to get back where you really belong."

For a moment he stared at her. Then: "Still the same Jeannie!" he said with his twisted smile. "No, my dear, there's no turning back for me. But if it comforts you, you're helping to keep me out of more trouble."

Was she? she wondered wearily. Or would the money only help to poison him more deeply. Would it have been better to refuse him a penny?

He said, pausing on his way to the door: "You won't forget the — thirty-first, isn't it?"

"No. I won't forget."

"What time will be most convenient for you to have me call?"

"Not before ten o'clock."

"Good. I'll be there. And — don't worry. That will be the last you'll see of me. Goodnight, and thank you."

"Don't make a noise, please," she requested softly. "There's a child asleep upstairs."

He nodded, and opening the front door, went out without another word. Jean shut the door quickly after him, hoping, as she bolted it again, that Tim would not hear. Moving noiselessly she cleared away the dirty sherry glass and the empty decanter before she went upstairs.

When she began to undress she remembered she had meant to ask McNairn how he had managed to trace her to the cottage. She little knew how relieved her late visitor was not to have been obliged to answer that awkward question. He had no wish to explain that it was his clever questioning of Tim that had sent him to London — with money borrowed from his friend at the inn — where more careful enquiries had put him in possession of her position at the hospital, and the length of time she had been there (he could still call on a natural charm, and had learnt various ways of getting information when he wanted it). In this case it had been obtained from the young under porter at St. Catherine's, who had innocently assured the person who enquired if a Sister named Jean Campbell was still there, as he was anxious to find her some time and thank her for all she had done for a wee bairn of whom the enquirer was very fond.

In his anxiety, that afternoon, over Jean's lateness in returning, Tim had entirely forgotten to mention the man who had brought back his ball. But what mattered to Jean now was her certainty that since McNairn had recognised her it was useless to try any longer to persuade herself that she was safe. She must either tell Blair the whole truth about herself, or break her engagement.

How crazy I am! she thought miserably. There is no "or" in it; I shall have to do both those things.

Unless she could simply end their relationship, by convincing him that she had made a mistake in thinking she cared enough to give up her career to marry him.

At the beginning she could have found the courage to make him listen to all the details of that old, tragic history; but when she thought of doing that now, her courage failed her, because she remembered that it would not only be the one stain on her name he would have to know about. In the face of what so many people had believed, would his faith in her be strong enough to make him believe in her complete innocence?

All the same, while she lay wide-eyed, hearing the Grandfather clock downstairs strike every hour of the night, she became more and more certain that she must tell Blair, whatever the price might be.

Chapter 9

I

At breakfast next morning it was difficult for Jean to appear her usual cheerful self. She had no appetite, and she was grateful that Tim's excitement over the picnic kept his attention fully occupied.

The small boy's attention was riveted on the sky where, through the sitting-room window, he could see the banks of cloud which were remorselessly blowing up from the west.

"Shan't we be able to go if it rains?" he asked anxiously. "Will —"

The question was cut short by the shrill ringing of the telephone bell. Jean rose at once, and telling Tim to get on with his breakfast, went out into the hall where the instrument stood.

While she lifted the telephone she was already sure that it must be Blair who was calling, and her heart was beating at a quickened tempo, even before she heard his voice.

"Is that you, Jean?" he asked.

"Yes — speaking."

"Darling! I have been trying to get you for ages, but there was some fault on the darned line," he told her.

"What is it?" she asked anxiously.

"An S.O.S. from Sir Rodney Henson. Apparently, he was trying to get through to me last night, and fortunately — or the other way — I kept my receptionist posted with my address here. It appears that the offspring of a Very Important Person is ill, and Sir Rodney, who is the great family's physician, wants me to go into a huddle over the case with him. I'm afraid it will mean the end of my holiday. And I can't even see you before I leave. There is only time to catch my train —"

How dreadful to feel actual relief! What a coward I am! she thought contemptuously, but her voice was steady when she told him:

"Of course you have to go. It's—hateful, and Tim will be devastated, poor child."

"Give him my love and tell him I'll see him in London. Could you come up a day or two earlier, and perhaps take him home with you?" Blair asked.

"I'll see."

"You do understand, don't you?"

"Of course I do. Oh, darling," Her tone was no longer steady, in that moment she could only remember he was going away. "Take great care of yourself," she begged.

"Of course. Take care of *your* precious self, and remember all the time that I love you—for ever. Dearest, I must go. By the way, I'm leaving the car—there's a man here who will bring it up at the end of the week. Meanwhile, it's at your service. Sweetheart, I must go. Remember!" He rang off.

Standing there, still holding the instrument, a wave of desolation swept over her, submerging that momentary relief. Was this to be the end of her dream? she asked herself. What would happen when they next met? . . .

II

Jean was still asking herself that question ten days later, while the train which was carrying herself and Tim back to London rushed on its way.

She had received several hastily written notes from Blair, and he had telephoned her twice since he left. But on resuming work a hundred things seemed to have caught up on him, and he told her that he had hardly a spare five minutes during the day. That meant that when he rang, it had to be at night, and as, after seven in the evening, the cottage and the few other telephones in its vicinity became a communal service—which meant anyone could listen in to anything that was said—it was impossible to carry on a private conversation. But Blair's letters had made up for their shortness in the warmth he put into them. In every one he had told her how he longed to be with her again; how empty everything seemed without her.

She knew that she should have kept to her resolution to write to him, telling him that she could not marry him; but though she had begun innumerable letters, she had not been able to bring herself to irrevocably shut the door on her happiness. She was telling herself now, with bitter self-contempt, that she was inexcusably weak for allowing herself to seize on the excuse that he was caught up in important work, and nothing should be done to disturb his mind at this juncture.

She had taken off her gloves, and as she looked down at her bare hands the sun caught the sapphire and diamonds of her engagement ring.

An almost unbearable pain pierced her heart. She knew that as long as she lived she would never forget the torture of these last days, each one of which had brought her nearer to the decision she could not make—and yet knew she must.

That Tim was unhappy, too, made things harder. He had hated leaving Cornwall, and clung to her more and more closely. But the time of parting was very near now; the little boy was being met at Paddington by John Barrington's secretary, and would be flown within a few hours to Monte Carlo, where his father had a villa.

They were travelling first class, and had a compartment to themselves. It did not improve Jean's spirits to see Tim in the seat opposite her, staring so unhappily out of the window.

"Tired, lovey?" she asked.

"No." He did not look round, and she knew that it would be best not to try to get him to talk just then. Best leave him; it would not help at all if they both broke down.

Taking Blair's most recent note from her bag she read it again.

"Darling," he had written under yesterday's date,

'I wish you had come back today. I shall be caught up all tomorrow with one thing and another, and in the

85

evening I must go to meet some darned foreign Professor at a dinner at Maynard-Phillips's. I seem to have appointments every minute until it will be time for that. It looks as though I can't see you until Friday, which is — need I tell you? — frustrating. Something seems to have happened to time! I'm even having to scrawl this in the car. Will you ring when I'm free? By the way, make up your mind to one thing definitely. We are going to be married by the end of this coming month. Matron already has plans in hand, to replace you. (Sorry, my sweet, but I was not going to wait for your return before telling her!) She will keep our guilty secret — seems to prefer it that way; I think she's nervous the infection that only wedding bells can cure, might spread. She says she is furious with me for stealing you, but is 'of a forgiving disposition'! Sweetheart, I will ring as soon as I get home tomorrow night, but I am afraid it will be too late to come and see you. It must be at least half a lifetime since I kissed you last, but at least there is the week-end to look forward to. I will tell you what arrangements I have made when we meet. Forgive a stupid scrawl, but it is all I can do under the circumstances. If I used all the notepaper in the world I could not tell you how much I miss you, and long to be with you again.

Until Friday — if it must be — and
Always,
Blair."

When she had read the note before leaving the cottage — the post had arrived almost at the same moment as the car which was taking Tim and herself to the station — the fact that Blair had told Matron of their engagement had hardly registered. But now, realising what he had done, she was filled with dismay. It was going to make everything so much more difficult.

"What's the matter, Jean? Are you unhappy too?"

Startled by the reminder of Tim's presence she looked across, and getting down from his seat he went and sat beside her, slipping a hot little hand into hers. "Shan't I see my Mr. Surgeon at all before going on the plane?" he enquired wistfully. "Not for a little minute?"

"I'm afraid not, darling," Jean told him. "He's very, very busy, looking after other little boys and girls. But he'll write to you."

"I hope so. Only it won't be really the same." The brown eyes that met hers were overbright. At rising seven Tim was both young and old for his age. His delicacy, having kept him away from the rough and tumble of school, had saved him from the rather awful over-sophistication which makes so many modern youngsters outgrow their childhood before they can begin to enjoy it. Seeing how near tears he was, Jean put a comforting arm round him.

"Listen, my precious," she said gently, "you are very nearly seven, and you must be a big, brave man. You must be very nice to Daddy, and show you love him best of any-one in the world, because he would feel very lonely if you didn't."

"I do love him," said Tim. "Only I love you and my — Mr. Marston too. Daddy's always so *busy*, and my Mummy never was there — much. Oh, I do wish you could come and live with us!"

She hugged him, her heart aching for this almost worse than motherless little person. "You're going to have a lovely time," she promised. "And soon you'll be learning lessons about all kinds of interesting things. And when Daddy brings you back to London, I'll be there, and we'll see each other often — "

Was that a cruel promise to make? she wondered suddenly. Would she be there? Not if she did what she ought to do; what, if she had not been so weak, she would already have done.

"And my Mr. Surgeon?" he urged.

"Oh, yes. He'll be there."

After a moment's silence Tim announced in his most grown-up manner:

"I've been thinking very seriously how nice it would be if you married my Mr. Surgeon, and I could come and live with you both whenever Daddy had to go away — What's the matter, Jean?" For he had felt her flinch.

"Nothing. That's only a fairy tale, you know, dear. Something nice to pretend about, but that will never happen," she said gently.

"Why not? I'm sure he'd like to marry you —"

"Well, I'm not going to marry anyone, and presently you will be going to school. When I'm old I might ask you to look after me. Or I will look after your children."

"Perhaps I won't have any children." Tim's built-in realism took over. "Anyhow, that wouldn't be nearly so nice. I suppose I shall have to marry you myself when I'm old enough."

The dull ache in her heart was suddenly almost unbearable. The years ahead! What could they bring? If she sent Blair away she knew nothing would ever fill the emptiness.

At Paddington Tim's escort collected him. He and Jean said their goodbyes before the train stopped, and determined not to be a crybaby he was keeping a stiff upper lip as far as possible.

But watching that now sturdy little figure disappear in the crowd, Jean's heart was heavy. Making Tim what he was today had been Blair's miracle in which she had been privileged to take a big part; and somehow the child would always seem a part of them both.

Then, aware that her porter was waiting, she followed him to a taxi.

Here she was, back in the great city where lay the work that had always meant so much to her. There were hundreds of other children who needed her help; the help she would always be ready to give. But coming back was not like it had been on other occasions; since she last saw London something had gone out of her life, and something had come into it.

She was sure she would never feel safe again. She actually dreaded meeting Blair, though all her love longed for the sight and touch of him again. But there could be no escape this time. What was she going to say to him? . . .

88

It was past six o'clock when she let herself into the flat where she lived, on the fourth floor of a block of modern service flats a few minutes' walk from the hospital.

Her home was a compact little suite of sitting-room, bed-room, and bathroom, with a small kitchenette where she could cook if she did not want to go down to the restaurant. The place was well looked after, and shiningly clean. It was her first home and she had loved it, but today, when she shut herself in after the porter who brought up her luggage had gone, she was conscious of a sense of loneliness.

When she came out of her bedroom, and was about to enter the kitchenette to make herself a cup of tea, she noticed the letter which had been put on the hall table. It was unstamped, and picking it up she studied the small, unusually distinct handwriting in which it was addressed, and felt again that curious sick fear which the memory of Neil McNairn brought to her.

She took it in with her, deliberately avoiding looking at it, while she filled the kettle and put it on.

Then, angry with herself, she snatched up the envelope and tore it open, skimming the few lines it contained.

"Just to say that things are getting rather urgent, and I'm hoping nothing has prevented your return today. Shall be along about 9 p.m. — earlier than arranged, but I have to keep an appointment at ten. Trust all is well with you.

As ever,
N. McNairn."

So here it was to greet her — that dark shadow stretching out to destroy her happiness.

She had sold out the bonds in which some of her savings were invested while she was in Cornwall, and had the cash with her. Once again, hating to feel that way, she was thankful that there was little chance of Blair coming to see her this evening.

She was drinking her tea when the doorbell pealed

sharply, and she started so violently that the liquid spilled over the table and her frock. Wiping it hurriedly she was in time to answer the second ring. It was not quite eight o'clock and she did not know what she had expected, but the sight of a messenger boy with a sheaf of roses wrapped in cellophane seemed almost an anti-climax.

She took the flowers, found a tip for the boy, and when she went back into the sitting-room the roses lay on the table where she had left them while she went for her bag. She undid the wrapping with trembling fingers and took the card out of the small envelope attached to the cellophane. *"With all my love and welcome back, darling. Ever, Blair."*

Jean pressed her face into the fragrance of the pink and crimson blossoms; she felt for a moment as though her love's arms were about her, and she was safe. Then in a wave of panic she thought: *I mustn't see him alone! I'm not strong enough to send him away!*

And what if he refused to be sent? That, too, was something she had to face.

The time of waiting seemed unending, and she was thankful when, just after nine, another ring sounded. Anxious only to get this over, she went to the door and found her unwanted visitor outside. Signing to him to enter, she shut the door again, and following her into the sitting-room McNairn said apologetically:

"I do hope I'm not putting you out, coming early?" Then: "How are you, Jean?"

"I have got what you want," she said, without replying to either of his questions. "If you will wait for a moment, I'll get it." She had already put the packet of notes in her small writing bureau, and taking them out she turned back to him.

Although it was barely twilight outside she had drawn the inner curtains and switched on the light. Now, looking at him directly for the first time she realised that he had been drinking. He was not drunk; he probably never did appear that way, but he was heavy-eyed and his careful speech a little blurred. What suddenly angered her was that he had done nothing to improve his appearance since she last saw him; if anything, he was even more down at heel. Then she noticed that he also looked ill, and the old liking she had once had for him stirred into fresh pity. She wanted to get rid of him as quickly as possible, and yet somehow she could not bring herself to tell him curtly to take his money and go.

Giving him the packet she said: "Won't you put that to some good use?" And added impulsively: "I wish I could feel you would pull yourself together."

"Maybe I will be able to," he replied. "Since you're so kind as to be interested, I have had a sort of opening. I might be able to go overseas. That could mean a fresh start. Do you believe in second chances?"

Somehow she could not let herself feel contempt at his tone. "Heaven knows I should," she replied. "I had mine, after all."

"Ah, but you deserved it. You're a wonderful person, Jeannie." This time there could be no doubting his sincerity. "I've been thinking about you a lot these last days. You must have worked so hard, and then I come along and — take a slice of what you've earned. But as Shakespeare says:

'*'Tis my necessity and not my will*
compels me —'

I — don't — like it. If you'll believe me. You're my country-woman, and —"

Realising he would soon arrive at the sentimental stage, she told him crisply: "Listen, please. I *have* worked very hard for what I have paid you. You must have some sense of honour, even if you have very little pride. Promise me that you won't spend any of that money on drink. If I thought it would make things worse for you, I should — hate it."

"Oh, I promise you it won't make things worse," he said. "So before I go, what about one last little doch-an-doris — for auld time's sake?" His wry, attractive smile coaxed her.

"Indeed not," she said firmly. "In any case I've nothing here. What you need," her manner was suddenly professional, "is a cup of strong coffee! I'll make you one. Sit down."

He obeyed meekly, pulling out a packet of cigarettes.

"May I smoke?" And when she told him he could, he said, "You won't even join me in that?"

"Not now." She left him, hoping that if he sobered up there might be more chance of his taking stock of himself; the nurse in her, who had learnt so much of the sins and weaknesses of her fellow humans, and the loyalty which was inborn in her, forced her more than half against her will to try to wake him to some sense of responsibility towards himself.

For whatever he was now, she reminded herself again that without him Jean Campbell could never have come into existence. And if his re-appearance in her life had crashed all chance of happiness, she was sure he would not have done that deliberately—if he were more responsible. She was too charitable and fair-minded to consider that he need never have reminded her of *his* existence.

But he knew it, and despised himself—even while he made the excuse that she wouldn't miss what he had taken, as she was going to marry Blair Marston.

A few minutes later, drinking a cup of the strong black coffee she brought him, he asked: "Would it be impertinence to wish you happiness, Jean? When will the wedding be?" He pointed to her ring.

With an instinctive movement she hid her hand. "There won't be a wedding," she said quietly. "Not now."

"Not? Why?" He looked suddenly alert.

"Need you ask? The man I was going to marry—I think I always knew I couldn't—knows nothing about Jean Stewart."

"Well, why should he?" McNairn bent towards her. "Jeannie, is it because I came to remind you, that you're thinking like this?"

"Not—altogether."

"Listen!" He had sobered now, and was serious. "If he doesn't know, *don't tell him*. Don't be a fool and throw your happiness away. The kind of happiness that counts so much! He loves you?"

"Yes," she admitted in a low voice. "But—"

"Then if you think it will make all that difference, ask

92

yourself: Have you any right to spoil *his* life—now wait! Listen to me—"

"I can't," she told him. "You don't understand. You are not the only person who knew Jean Stewart. Supposing I married Blair and someone found out—about what happened? You should understand that a doctor can't afford a scandal."

"You're just being absurd," he said, his speech no longer blurred, his eyes steadily on hers. "*I* knew you—but that's different. Who in the world would connect that unhappy girl of not eighteen with the respected Nursing Sister Jean Campbell? No one. You were always a sonsie lass, Jean, and you're beautiful now. No one from the old days would recognise you. The secret is between you and me, and it's buried."

She shook her head. "The ghost of it is there—in my life. I won't marry Blair without telling him, and I can't do that because—Oh, you've forgotten what all those people believed. Some of them, like the jury, may have doubted my guilt on the main charge. But how many believed that Ronald Cardine was not my lover? I couldn't bear to have Blair think that."

"He wouldn't. And if he did, it was all so long ago, and values have changed." McNairn urged. "He wouldn't hold it against you. Forget all that; forget the whole thing. I've seen your man. He's a fine type, and isn't he the single-minded kind? Dedicated?"

"Yes."

"Jean, I'll tell you something," he said earnestly. "There are men who love only one woman in their lives. Not many, perhaps, but it happens. If Blair Marston is that kind, you'd be taking the mainspring of his existence away. Have you any right to risk condemning him to that?"

She looked at him uncertainly, hardly able to believe that he, who in such different days had been looked on as a cynic, could speak like this—as if a man's need for love was something he understood. But before she could make any reply, McNairn rose.

"I'll be on my way," he said. "Thank you, lassie. And

remember what I've said. It's only between you and me now — no one else will ever know. Don't throw your happiness away. And I'll do my best to deserve your help."

Going out to the front door he opened it and turned, holding out his hand. "I'll try to behave myself. Here's my hand on it."

She gave him her own. "Goodbye." Then as she heard the lift along the passage stop and the clang of opening gates she drew him back with a hasty: "Wait a minute." She had remembered that a member of the hospital committee had a flat on this floor, and the last thing she wanted was to be seen letting a man out of her own flat — especially a somewhat disreputable specimen like this one.

Quick enough to realise that, her visitor would have followed her in again, but the person who had come out of the lift was already almost at the door.

"Jean —" Blair broke off, looking enquiringly from her whitened face to her companion, while, trying to hide her horror she could only stammer:

"Blair! I — wasn't expecting —" Her voice trailed away, and there was a deadly little pause.

Chapter 10

I

It could be counted to Neil McNairn's credit, whatever his faults were, that he was as dismayed as Jean herself. Then almost immediately the submerged man of the world in him reacted to the situation, and doing his best to cover Jean's dismayed silence, he said easily:

"Are you not going to introduce me, Jeannie?"

The training she had momentarily forgotten coming to her help, she recovered outwardly at once.

"Of course. Blair, this is Mr. McNairn — An old friend of mine — Mr. Marston."

"How are you?" The Scotsman shook hands cordially. "I was passing through London, and I thought I must look the wee Jeannie up," he continued. "She'll always be wee Jeannie to me. I've known her long since."

"Really?" Blair sounded coldly polite.

The other man nodded. "Yes. She's gone a long way these last years; she's a good lassie and a clever one. I hear she's going to marry you, and believe me you're a lucky fellow, Mr. Marston. All happiness to you both." He lifted a wrist with a flourish, disclosing a frayed cuff, and dropping his hand hastily asked: "Could you tell me the time? My watch is being cleaned and I'm all at sea without it."

"It's a quarter past ten," Blair told him.

"Is it! I must be on my way, or I'll miss my train. Goodbye, Jean — Goodbye, Professor." He gave Blair a friendly nod. "Maybe we'll meet again. Take care of yourself, honey." And patting Jean's shoulder he set his hat at a jaunty angle and strode away.

But any relief Jean might have felt at getting rid of her

95

most unwelcome guest was cancelled out by her secret dismay. McNairn was the last person she had wanted Blair to meet.

Then taking her hand he drew her inside the flat and shut the door, telling her: "I managed to get away earlier than I expected, darling. So I came without waiting to telephone, hoping to find you still up. Are you really here?" He drew her towards him. "Do you realise it is twelve whole days since I kissed you?"

With his lips on hers, the consciousness of his nearness in every pulse beat, she knew that she had been crazy to believe that she could send him away. Whatever the future held, there must be some way out.

When he released her, flushed and a little breathless, she raised her shining eyes to his. "I didn't expect you. I thought it would be too late — "

"The learned Professor took himself off to bed; he has a plane to catch in the morning. So I came along — to find you entertaining another man!" He looked at her in quizzical disapproval. "Tell me, please — *who* is the elderly boy friend?"

"I have known him since I was in my teens." She would have been happier without the relief knowing that was true brought to her. "He called — and I couldn't refuse to let him in, could I?"

"I suppose not. But would it be hurtful to say I hope he doesn't come back? Or do you like him?"

She turned to the table, lifting the tray which contained the coffee pot and used cup. "He once did me a good turn." She was grateful for the steadiness of her voice. "Shall I make you some fresh coffee?"

"No thanks. Do you mind if I open the window, darling. The room smells like a bar! Have you been celebrating auld lang syne?"

"He only had coffee with me. Yes, open the window." She went quickly along to the kitchenette, and glad to be alone for a few moments, paused by the stove. She ought to tell him — now! She ought to send him away —

Then thrusting back the knowledge that there could be no

other way, came the echo of McNairn's voice, with that unmistakably sincere conviction in it: *"There are men who love only one woman in their lives . . . you'd be taking the mainspring of his existence away . . . Have you any right to risk condemning him to that . . . It's only between you and me now"* . . .

Pressing her hands to her throbbing temples she asked herself yet again: *"What shall I do?"*

"Where have you got to, darling?" Blair called. "Come back here. I want to tell you something."

"Coming." But it was a few moments before she could summon enough courage to return to him. Taking her hand he drew her down to sit beside him on the sofa. Then noticing her pallor and the dark marks under her eyes his smile faded.

"Darlingest!" he exclaimed. "You're worn out! What a selfish devil I am, coming along and keeping you up — quite forgetting you had been travelling most of the day. You must go straight to bed the moment you've shut me out — which will be very quickly now."

"No, don't go," she said, a sudden dread of losing him swamping all other feelings. "I'm — wide awake."

"Then you will take something to make you sleep. Because being — as I pointed out just now — a selfish devil — "

"Blair! What nonsense. You!"

"Yes, me!" He put one of the hands he still held to his lips. "Hear the worst before you get indignant. You must have a good night, because tomorrow morning I am going to collect you and take you down into the country — you can't say No. My mother is expecting us, and tomorrow and Sunday will be your last really free days before you plunge back into work. I have arranged — somehow! — to keep this week-end; it has, as you will have gathered from my letters, been murder lately."

"Blair, you haven't told your mother that — " She broke off, staring at him in dismay.

"That I want her to meet her future daughter-in-law? Certainly I have. She sent you her best love and is longing to meet you. As a matter of fact," he added, laughing, "she has heard a good deal about you for some time past. It

97

appears that when I've been with her, your name has been mentioned rather oftener than I meant it to be! Anyway, we are due at Arleigh Hall for what is left of the week-end." He rose. "And now, having broken the worst to you, I'm off."

"But—I can't go!" she protested. "Dearest, don't you realise that I've a great deal to do—things that must be put in order over this week-end? I've been away for a month, and—Oh, you should have told me earlier."

"Sorry, darling. But it's arranged, and we can't possibly back out now. It will be a very quiet party. My sister is coming to stay while her husband is abroad—Mama will have told her our news now, and she'll be all agog to meet you. You really won't find my people a frightful ordeal, I promise. They'll adore you. So—be ready for me in the morning, won't you?"

She said reproachfully, "I thought you agreed to keep our engagement quiet for a little while longer."

"But why on earth should we have done?" He sounded slightly impatient. "I want to tell all the world—and I mean to!"

It was too late to make any further protest. She knew that she could not possibly let him down now; whatever came of it, she would have to fall in with the arrangements he had made. But when, later, his arms closed about her while he bent to kiss her goodnight, she suddenly felt trapped. The feeling passed quickly, though, and was replaced by a new fatalism.

If this was the way things were meant to go, why reject the gifts the gods offered? McNairn could so easily be right —there was a chance in a million of anyone else connecting the girl who was going to marry Blair Marston with that other Jean.

II

Blair had a small bachelor flat a few minutes' walk from his consulting rooms in Harley Street. After leaving Jean he decided to walk home; he was not using his car that evening, and had arrived at Jean's in a taxi. It was a perfect night. The London sky, which of late years has become so blessedly free of the smoke pall which used to dim it even in the clearest weather, made a dark sapphire canopy above the West End. A still young moon hung over the east; and turning from the main thoroughfares into the quieter streets of the Doctors' Quarter, he strode along smoking a cigar, his thoughts free of every subject but one.

However fully occupied he had been since his return to London, Jean had never been completely expelled from his mind. He would have asked: How could she be, when she was so completely a part of him? Yet it was only now, since he had seen and touched her again, that he knew how lonely he had been. He hoped that his decision to override her wish to postpone the announcement of their engagement a little longer had not upset her. It was characteristic of him to take the direct road to anything he wanted, and thinking it over, he had been sure that her reluctance to make their relationship known was simply part of that curious reserve which he had found it so difficult to get through. It was strange, he mused, that anyone with Jean's experience should retain that core of shyness — for he was sure that was what it was.

Bless her! he was glad he had spiked her guns. And having gone so far he was determined to see that the notice of their engagement should be sent to the papers. What the dickens did it matter if her fellow nurses chattered! Then remembering, rather ruefully, his own wish for a quiet wedding, he laughed to himself. It did not look as though that would be as possible as both he and Jean had hoped. He was quite sure his mother was already making the, to her mind necessary, plans. They could be married in the village church where he had been christened! Being over fifty miles from London, that might make the darned crowd smaller.

He had almost reached the block where he lived when a mini-saloon coming in the same direction passed him and with a screech of brakes hurriedly applied, drew into the kerb just ahead of him and stopped. Nobody got out, and, decidedly disapproving of what he considered careless driving, Blair glanced frowningly at the car, and with a mental shrug rather regrettably decided: *Woman driver!*

He was striding by when the nearside door was thrust open and a familiar voice called softly:

"Oi! Are you going to cut me?"

He stopped, turning quickly towards the slender figure who had alighted.

"Lorna! What on earth are you doing here?"

"I've been to the world's dullest party!" his cousin announced. "Where are you off to? Home to bed like a good boy?"

"Home, anyway," he replied.

"You are not going to work, or anything like that at this hour?"

"No."

"Shall I confess," she asked, "that I was wondering if I dared call on you without ruining your reputation?"

He laughed. "Are you as dangerous as that?"

"Not to you, dear. I wonder—would you like to be kind and give me a drink? I assure you I won't be qualifying for a breathalyser on the way home! The people I was dining with—friends of my Papa's—must be practically T.T.'s!"

"And what would Uncle Simon say if he knew I was encouraging you to go the other way?" he asked.

"Oh, Daddy gave me up years ago," she retorted.

"I believe he did. O.K., come along in."

She had stopped a bare half dozen yards from the entrance to the flats where he lived and, locking the car, she walked the short distance beside him.

At any other time he might have found an excuse not to ask her in, but tonight he felt relaxed and happy—in the mood to be tolerant to all the world. Besides, taken all in all, he had a certain amount of careless affection for Lorna; it was no more than a clannish family thing—he was extremely fond of her father—and it would never have remotely occurred to him that her interest was any warmer than his own.

They went up in the lift to the third floor, and a few moments later he left her, to collect ice for their drinks; Lorna had announced that she wanted something "long and cool".

Waiting for him, she glanced about her. She had been here before, though not for some months, and she found the restful room with its well filled bookcases and deep leather covered chairs not altogether to her taste.

The kind of half study he would have wherever he lived, she supposed. Very masculine. She entirely missed the gracious beauty of the pieces of antique furniture, some of which had come from Blair's mother's house, others that, a connoisseur in such things, he had picked up with loving care. But Lorna's taste ran to ultra-modern décor, and she decided that one day he would have to change all this for a house, or a much larger flat; the kind of home where a very successful surgeon would entertain the kind of people who would be useful in pushing his career still further. She had always been determined that, however long she had to wait, she would ultimately be the girl he would settle down with; for she had a favourite theory that any girl could get the man she wanted if she knew how to set about it, and was determined enough.

True, Blair had never shown any signs of marrying, but that had been something to be grateful for, and she was certain she would succeed sooner or later. They were always meeting at his mother's house, and when she got herself into the hospital she had hoped to see a great deal more of him; if that had not turned out quite as she planned, it irritated more than dismayed her. But though she had such strong faith in her particular brand of sex-appeal, she quite left out the fact that it might leave Blair stone cold. She was not at all satisfied, though, with the small amount she had lately seen of him outside the hospital; she had hoped that when he was on holiday he might spend some time in Suffolk, but instead he had gone off, heaven knew where. His mother had been vague, apart from saying he was "somewhere in the West Country".

When Lorna first went to St. Catherine's he had some-times taken her out to dinner and the odd theatre, but for quite a time now she had seen less and less of him. Anyhow, for these last weeks at least, Sister Jean Campbell had been off the scene. Thinking that now, and then remembering Jean would be back in the ward on Monday, Lorna frowned, biting her lips. She would certainly have to do something about that so-and-so of a girl! There was no doubt that Blair was interested in his marvellously efficient Sister-in-Charge.

The scheming snake! Lorna thought viciously. If she thinks she's going to get him, she's very much mistaken! Reaching for a box of cigarettes on the walnut table at her elbow, she knocked over a framed photograph that was standing near it, and in the act of replacing it paused abruptly, staring down at the picture the leather frame contained. Obviously an enlarged snap-shot—the picture of a girl sitting on the grass against the background of a creeper-covered cottage, her arm round a small boy while they both laughed into the camera.

Jean and Tim Barrington! Where had it been taken, and what was it doing in Blair's sitting-room? Then hearing him return, she hastily put the frame down.

"Sorry I've been so long. I had to get the darned ice," Blair apologised. "Are you passing out?"

She laughed. "I've managed to survive."

"Good." He mixed her a gin sling, and taking the glass from him she held it up.

"Well, here's to you—Stranger!"

"Why stranger?"

"No one sees you any more."

"Nonsense." He poured out his own drink and sat down opposite her. "You see me every day—except Sundays."

"Only in duty hours. Don't you ever go down to Arleigh?"

"My dear girl," he protested, "I've been away. And since I've come back I have hardly had time to turn round. I'm going down tomorrow, though."

"Oh, are you? I was wondering whether Aunt Harriet could do with me this week-end," she said casually.

"I rather fancy she's going to be full up."

"What—a house party?"

He shrugged. "Human various. Anyway, I'm taking a friend down."

"A friend?"

"Um."

Don't be silly! Lorna told herself. *It isn't likely. She's away.* Or—wasn't it likely? She looked down at her glass, her eyes narrowing. Then glancing up, she said frankly: "You know, Blair, I miss you a lot. We used to at least see something of each other, and I hoped we were—chums."

"There's hardly time to see anyone, these hectic days," he replied, smiling. "I'm pretty well caught up, and likely to be more so."

There was a moment's silence. Then realising he was looking at the photograph which had roused her angry curiosity, she could no longer restrain herself.

"That's surely Sister Campbell and the Barrington kid," she said. "Did she give it to you?"

"She did not." Blair helped himself to a cigarette, and with a quick apology offered her the box. Lighting hers he said casually: "As a matter of fact, I took that picture. Down in Cornwall."

It was all she could do to manage to bite back an angry exclamation. But only she was conscious of how electrical the brief silence was. Then:

"What on earth was young Tim doing with Sister in Cornwall?" she asked. "And—if it's not unduly inquisitive, how come that you were there?"

"Oh, that's quite a story." He sounded amused. *He looks,* Lorna thought furiously, *like the cat who's swallowed the cream!* He continued: "Tim couldn't go where it had been arranged he should, because there was infection in the house—measles. And as his father had to go abroad, Jean, being a saint, took charge of him while she was on holiday. As I was in the fairly near neighbourhood I took the opportunity to have a look at the boy. That, by the way," he nodded towards the photograph, "was just a snap I had enlarged. It's rather a good one of Jean."

Jean! Lorna was almost choking with rage, but she managed to ask quite naturally: "And did you see much of Sister Campbell and her charge?"

"Oh, yes, quite a lot." Serenely unaware of the storm he was raising, but realising that his instinctive use of Jean's first name had suggested more than a professional acquaintanceship, Blair determined that there should be no misunderstanding. Since after this week-end she would be bound to hear of his engagement, there seemed no reason why he should not tell his cousin right away. While he paused, Lorna's short, rather breathless laugh cut across his thoughts.

"Blair, my precious innocent, I do hope Sister was not living alone with the child."

"Of course she was. Why not?" He looked back at her with surprise which held just the dawn of displeasure.

"Why not?" she repeated, her tone suddenly brittle. "Don't you realise the gossip and scandal there would be in the hospital if it came out that you were—on rather intimate terms with Sister Campbell! It's no use frowning and telling me it's no one's business. In these days no one would believe for an instant that you went to see the *boy*. They'd say you and Sister—" She finished the sentence with a shrug.

"They won't have a chance of saying it," Blair told her calmly. "If they want something to talk about they will have it, no doubt, when they hear that 'Sister Campbell' and I are going to be married."

"It's not true!" The exclamation was wrung from her before she could stop it, as she sprang to her feet, too shattered to choose her words. "Blair, you can't be going to marry that—that girl! Who is she? What is she? No one really knows anything about her background; she is the most secretive creature. Oh, you *can't!*"

Even the most brilliant masculine minds are often far more innocent than feminine ones. Blair could not understand why his announcement should have been received like this, but as he met Lorna's furious eyes, anger sparked in his own. He said coldly:

"This is nonsense. Why on earth, because she does not take all and sundry into her confidence, should Jean be 'secretive'? Anyhow, she has done me the great honour of promising to be my wife, and the more people who know about it, and the sooner they know, the better. Apart from Matron and my mother, you are the first person to be told. Surely you are going to wish me happiness?"

She already realised her mistake. This was not the way to get what she wanted. Her expression changed, though her eyes remained hard as she held out both hands to him.

"Dearest Blair, of course I wish you happiness. Do forgive me. It was such a shock—I've never thought of you marrying, and I suppose I should never consider anyone quite good enough for you. I hope she realises what a lucky, lucky girl she is!"

"The luck is all on my side." He took her hands and briefly kissed the cheek she offered.

She turned away, and picking up her glass, drained it and held it out to him. "I think another drink is indicated, then I must go. Something short this time."

While he mixed it she had time to pull herself together, and when he turned back to her she managed to smile naturally. "You know," she told him again, "somehow I never thought of you as a marrying man."

He laughed. "Aren't we all? When the right person comes along."

Lorna swallowed her rage with an effort. *The right person!* But she too, had been trained to self-control in an emergency, and this was, she felt, the worst she had ever encountered. How to handle it needed a lot of thought!

Finishing her drink she rose. "Well, I hope you have all the luck in the world," she told him. "Thanks for the alcohol—I don't think I've qualified for that breathalyser—hope not, anyway! Wouldn't Matron be livid!"

"You're O.K. See you on Monday then." He went

down to the outside door with her, and going up again through the quiet building, forgot all about her.

But Lorna, driving in the direction of the nurses' hostel, remembered him, and was seething with rage and disappointment.

That bitch Jean Campbell! Of course, with her quiet, sly ways she had schemed to get him from the beginning! Blair could not be allowed to marry her—but how could he be stopped?

As Lorna began to examine the situation a little more coolly, commonsense and her knowledge of her cousin's character told her that any show of antagonism would be the last thing to succeed. Surely, there must be some way round this thing which threatened to upset all her cherished plans for her own future—and Blair's. . . .

III

On the following day, while Blair's car turned from the busy main road, along the winding Suffolk lanes by which his mother's house was reached, Jean was wondering apprehensively what awaited her at the end of this drive.

The beauty of the countryside in high summer lay all about them. At any other time it would have enchanted her; she would have felt that she really had reached the haven of all those dreams which she had been so sure would never come true.

If only she could still her nagging conscience; or bring herself to insist on Blair hearing her story! Never had she thought it possible to be so torn in half as she was being now. Yet all the time, forcing itself upon her, there remained the echo of McNairn's voice, like some tempting Lucifer, insisting that she had no right to spoil Blair's happiness.

"At last!"

She came out of her unhappy reverie with a jerk, and looking round, met the smiling warmth of her companion's eyes.

"What, darling?" she asked.

He laughed. "You were half asleep."

"No. Just—thinking. Had you been talking to me?" She was grateful that, approaching a bend, he was obliged to watch the road.

"No. But I was going to say: At last I am taking you where I have always wanted to. Remember when I asked you to let me bring you to meet my mother, in the hospital that day? Only to be quietly but firmly put in my place!"

"Oh, dearest, no!" she protested. "If I was not—enthusiastic, it was not because I didn't want to come. Only because—" She broke off, remembering too well all her reasons for being sure she must not accept even his friendship.

"Because you felt you did not want to encourage me!" He laughed, moving one hand from the wheel to lay it briefly over hers.

She made no reply. Did she not know how right she had been? Even now it was impossible to completely repress the nagging question at the back of her mind: *If he knew*, would he ever have wanted to bring her to meet his mother? And here she was, still grasping the happiness to which she felt she had no right. Still drifting; still trying to cling to something which she was sure in her heart she should forego.

But how she longed to see the man she loved in the environment to which he had belonged all his life. She knew Blair was devoted to his mother, and that up to now her house had always been the place he called home.

Then suddenly they were turning through a white gate which had been hospitably fastened back. They travelled perhaps a hundred yards in the shade of overhanging trees, and came in sight of a long, low, gabled house over which masses of purple clematis and climbing roses grew in lovely profusion.

Arleigh Hall was not a large house, but it was a superb specimen of its kind. Originally a farm, Jean knew from

what her beloved had told her that it had been in the
Marston family for the last three hundred years, and that
the family had very deep roots in the county. Until the
Hall had come into possession of Blair's father—who was a
younger son—the owners had concentrated exclusively on
farming the land. But Blair's father had broken the tradi-
tion, because before the unexpected death of his elder
brother, he had become a doctor—and as a country
practitioner was loved throughout the neighbourhood,
where his practice had stretched over many miles, taking
in several villages. He had died three years ago. Much
of the agricultural land, and the two small farms on it,
were let now; and the family was very far from rich—not
that they ever had been, as riches go in these days,
and taxation, death duties and all the robberies to which
governments are prone had made them considerably
poorer.

When the car stopped before the wide open front door,
Mrs. Marston came swiftly out to meet them. Slender and
upright, with closely curling white hair, she still kept far
more than just the remainder of, if not strict beauty,
something that was more than mere prettiness. And at
once Jean knew where Blair had got his handsome eyes
and that keen straight glance that was such a strong
characteristic.

"So this is Jean! A thousand welcomes, my dear." That
intent stare, too warm to be disconcerting, held the younger
woman's for a moment, while Mrs. Marston's small,
capable hands closed firmly on those she had taken. Then
turning to her son with a smiling nod, she announced:
"She'll do!" And having embraced him fondly, she invited:
"Come along in, both of you."

The loneliness and insecurity which had dogged Jean for
so long, seemed to melt away in the warmth of that welcome. For the first time since her childhood she had a
sense of belonging as she went into the house, one hand in
Blair's, the other held by his mother.

Looking back on it afterwards, that day always seemed
like some lovely green oasis; so hedged in with comfort and

security, that there could be no thought of any desert encroaching on it. From the first moment it seemed so natural to be here—to think of Blair's home as hers.

Mrs. Marston carried her off to her own sanctum after tea, while Blair went to pay expected visits to the local doctor, and the Vicar, who had both known him since he was a small boy.

"My dear," the elder woman confided, "I can't tell you how happy it makes me to know that you and Blair are going to marry. For a long time I have been so absolutely certain you were the right girl for him."

"A long time?" Jean looked at her enquiringly.

Mrs. Marston nodded. "Oh, he doesn't keep secrets from his Mum!" she assured laughingly. "I know at once when he is worried or unhappy. Believe me, I heard a lot about you; so much, that I guessed before he admitted it, you were the girl I had always hoped he would find. Though I must say, I was *not* so pleased when I realised you were— holding out on him."

"Did he tell you that?" Jean asked quickly.

"No, my dear. I just knew it. I told him to bring you down here, but the answer to that was, that you had made him understand you did not want to come."

"Oh, was I as ungracious as that!" exclaimed Jean. "I did want to come, but—" She broke off, biting her lip. How impossible it was to explain.

"Perhaps you were frightened of letting yourself get involved," said Mrs. Marston. "You do love him, don't you? You will make him happy?"

"That is all I want to do in the world. If I was—if I had been sure of that—" Jean stopped again, and the elder woman helped her out.

"You were not sure that you wanted to give up your profession. But I am certain you were born for each other," she added firmly.

Remembering that later, while she undressed, Jean thought: surely this lovely thing which had come to her had been meant to happen; compensation for all the misery and the lonely years which had robbed her of those things youth has a right to. And to refuse to accept the gift of Blair's love would be base ingratitude. After all, had not Mrs. Marston repeated almost word for word what McNairn had impressed so urgently on her?

Chapter 11

I

Even if the bright sunlight and that new, wonderful sense of feeling so welcome, had not helped to scare Jean's bogies away, there was not much time to think beyond the happenings of the next day.

In the morning she went to church with Mrs. Marston and Blair, and though it was rather an ordeal to know that it was she, rather than the Vicar's sermon, that held the interest of the congregation, she managed to appear unconscious of the many curious glances of the villagers. And not only the villagers. There were people from the big houses round, and after the service she was introduced to Sir James and Lady Drummond, who were the Hall's nearest neighbours.

Sir James, it appeared, was a J.P., and his wife the head of the local branch of the Women's Institute. Rather to Jean's relief, the Drummonds were in a hurry, and promising "dear Harriet" (Blair's Mama) that they would look her up later, they drove off.

"Darling, I am afraid you have been stared out of countenance!" Blair said apologetically, afterwards. "You must forgive the natural curiosity. Most people here have known me since I was in my pram, and no doubt their interest started earlier than my first appearance in their midst!" He glanced mischievously at his mother.

"Oh, yes!" she agreed. "The older inhabitants were eager to know whether I was going to produce a son or a daughter!"

Back at the house Blair's sister Annette, awaited them. It was Jean's first meeting with Annette Fairleigh, who lived in the West Country since her marriage; the two girls liked each other on sight, and again Jean felt that she was completely accepted.

Some neighbours called in the afternoon, and by the time they went, it was also time to change for dinner.

Following his young woman to the bottom of the stairs Blair asked a little discontentedly: "Can you hurry over the unnecessary effort to make yourself lovelier, dearest? I don't seem to have exchanged two words with you since lunch."

"I'll be down in twenty minutes," she promised.

"Splendid girl!" he approved. "I'll beat you to it." And sure enough he was waiting when she went downstairs again.

Slipping an arm through hers he led her into the empty drawing-room. "There is something I want to ask you, sweetheart," he said. "Before I say anything to my Mama!"

She looked up at him enquiringly. "Yes — ?"

He bent to kiss her, then still holding her against him, explained: "When I told my mother we wanted a really quiet wedding, she immediately suggested that if we did not want a lot of fuss in London, it would be a good idea to get married down here. I had been thinking the same. Could you bear to do that?"

Her heart missed a beat, and meeting her startled glance he asked: "What is the matter, darling? Do you hate the thought? It would keep the journalists away, and we need only ask a few people — well, comparatively few. My mother threatens 'never to forgive me' if I do her — and yourself — out of a real wedding!"

"Of course I don't hate it. A country wedding is lovely." Jean managed to sound natural, although the doubt that remained like a coiled snake at the back of her mind had raised its head again.

"Then we arrange it that way," said Blair.

If it was for his happiness! If she only knew that her weakness — for it was characteristic of her to call it that — would never bring harm to him.

"Darling heart." Blair drew her close again. "Please don't look so serious. This is a *wedding* we're discussing!"

Her heart leapt beneath his hand, and with his lips on hers that wonderful sense of safety returned to her. Then as the sound of voices in the hall called them back to the knowledge that there were other people in the world, Blair released her, and they turned to greet his mother and Annette as they came into the room.

II

During dinner Mrs. Marston and Annette, who were both delighted at the idea of the wedding taking place at Polsford church, discussed arrangements for it throughout the meal.

"Thank goodness there are not hordes of relatives we have to be careful not to offend by forgetting them—and who, when they do exist, always send the wrong presents!" Annette laughed. "There's only Uncle Leo, Mummy—my solitary uncle, who is rather a poppet, Jean. He'll be cock-a-hoop over your marrying at last, Blair, and will certainly fall for Jean."

"You must let us have a list of the people you want, dear," said Mrs. Marston.

"Thank you, but there's nobody," Jean replied. "You see, if I asked any of the girls from the hospital, it would only mean heart-burnings for those who were left out."

"Of course, Matron will come—that's a must," Blair observed, seeing the sudden shadow in Jean's eyes and sensing that she did not want her friendlessness to be highlighted.

"But surely there's someone in Scotland—" began Annette.

"No one," Jean answered quietly. "The only person up there who would be interested, couldn't possibly travel so far."

"What about bridesmaids?" asked Mrs. Marsden.

Annette looked at Jean. "Will you have me as Matron of Honour? And Oh! what about Lorna!" A slightly dismayed note crept into her voice. "She's on your staff, isn't she? Are you great friends?"

113

Jean hesitated, finding the question decidedly embarrassing, and Blair said, giving her a quizzical look:

"Jean is much too kind to tell you that Lorna is rather more of a liability than an asset; she is too sweet to suggest that, even to me! Good heavens, Anne, are you suggesting *Lorna* should be a bridesmaid?"

"Well," Annette sounded less confident. "I think she may be hurt if she isn't asked."

"How do you feel about that, darling?" Blair looked at his fiancée.

"I suppose it depends on how Lorna feels," she answered with more serenity than she felt. "But—do I really need bridesmaids? I should love it if Annette will be my Matron of Honour, but I don't want a whole bevy of attendants!"

"Well, dear, perhaps it can be arranged," Mrs. Marston agreed. "But a lovely frock you must have—that is going to be part of my present. I shall come up to town next week, and we will go to Julian Lorrimer for it. He made Annette's, and he really is good."

"How terribly kind of you." Jean flushed. "Only I thought—something very simple."

"Nonsense. It's your day, and you must look the part. She'll make a delightful bride, Blair. Don't let her argue."

"Hear that? I crack the whip here!" Blair laughed indulgently. "I suppose all I'm really allowed to do is to wait in the wings. But you're beginning to make me feel nervous already, Mama!"

"Rubbish!" she retorted. "It will be wonderful. And however we limit our lists, the whole village will turn out *en masse*, so we must give them a really good show."

By the time they left the table it had been decided that the wedding would take place before the end of the month, though no definite date would be set until Jean left the hospital.

Pausing in the hall before following the others into the drawing-room, Blair told his beloved a little ruefully: "I'm afraid we shall have to let the little Mum take over the stage management, darling. We're completely in her hands now. Never mind!" He smiled mischievously down at her. "It's only 'once in a lifetime'—in ours, anyway."

She nodded. Somehow it was strangely comforting to feel that events were now beyond her control. All the time her conscience and her longing to snatch her happiness had pulled against each other, but now it seemed as though whatever destiny controlled her life had taken everything out of her hands, and she was almost feverishly determined to no longer look back.

Mrs. Marston was pouring out the coffee when they joined her. The drawing-room was a charming apartment, with that air of being part of a home which characterised the whole house. White walls against which crystal electric sconces glowed behind pale rose coloured shades; a rose coloured carpet made the background for beautiful pieces of antique furniture in burr walnut, and deeply cushioned chairs covered with brocade of a delicately flowered pattern.

It was still light outside, and the long windows were wide open. Blair brought Jean her coffee, and having fetched his own, lowered himself into a chair beside her. Annette, who had not seen her brother for some time, had plenty to say to him, and not feeling in the least out of it Jean was content to listen to the family—*her* family—gossip.

It was this happy circle that was broken up by the sound of a step on the loggia outside the french windows, and a voice exclaiming:

"Hello, people! Am I in time for some coffee? I've walked miles, and I'm parched!"

"Lorna! Where on earth have you come from?" asked Mrs. Marston, presenting a cheek for her niece's kiss as Lorna came quickly into the room and bent over her. If she was not too pleased, she showed no sign of it.

Lorna said, dividing a smile between her aunt and Blair: "I knew these people would be here. I'm with the Egertons at Stavely St. Mary. They were up in town for a party yesterday, and drove me down afterwards." She glanced at Jean. "No one need look disapproving. It's my free Sunday, and I shall be back on duty in time—though I'll have to leave at the crack of dawn. I just had to come and have a look at you two! Jean, I do wish you all the happiness in the world. Clever girl! Persuading the family bachelor to become a Benedict!" She sounded warmly amused, but as their eyes met, Jean saw that the other girl's were as cold as ice, and knew how right she had been. Lorna was not pleased; but how could she have found out? She looked quickly at Blair, and in answer to her unspoken question he said:

"I forgot to tell you, darling, I broke the good news to Lorna yesterday, when we had a drink together."

Turning to her aunt again, Miss Temple rattled on gaily: "What do you think of it all, darling? Isn't it marvellous?"

"I could not be happier," Mrs. Marston assured.

Lorna nodded. "But what a dark horse you are, Jean. I don't have to call you 'Sister' when we are on the brink of being cousins, do I?"

"Of course not," agreed Jean. "But didn't Blair tell you we had decided not to broadcast it in the hospital? Of course, Matron knows. But, *please*, no one else."

"Oh, Lorna won't talk. Will you ring for another cup, Blair?" said Mrs. Marston.

For a moment Lorna watched him as he crossed the room, her eyes narrowed. Then she flashed another smile at Jean. "You've got to make him terribly happy, or I'll slay you! He's my very favourite person—"

"Of course she will. She's the right girl to do it," Mrs. Marston said incisively.

Lorna laughed. "You remind me of Blair when he's extra determined. But of course she will." If she was aware of how unwelcome she was, she showed no sign of being anything but completely at her ease. And when presently Blair gave her her coffee cup, she remained in the chair next to Jean, which she had taken, apparently quite at home.

"Did you really walk over from the Egertons?" her aunt asked.

"Yes. I came across the fields. A crowd of people had turned up, and I told Cynthia I'd just take the opportunity to slip over here. I shan't say no if Blair offers to drive me back."

"Is that so?" His tone was non-committal.

Turning to Jean Lorna asked: "When are you going to desert the hospital for one of its chief Consultants? There will be discontent about whoever gets your job. Not that I'm after it! In fact, I am thinking of going over to private nursing."

"Why not give it up altogether?" Blair asked coolly.

"Am I so very bad?" Her expression was reproachful.

Jean said quietly, "Of course you are not bad, and you could be that little more than just good—if you would."

"When I feel like it, you mean? Anyway, I don't think I'll risk the disapproval of whoever takes over from you," said Lorna. "Cinderella will certainly miss you, Jean." If it was grudging, there was a certain amount of sincerity in the remark. Anyhow, Lorna felt that few Sisters would have been as patient with her as Jean had been.

Jean, determined to establish as pleasant a relationship as possible with Blair's cousin, said: "We're going to have a very quiet wedding, but we were wondering just now if you could bear to be a bridesmaid, Lorna."

"Me? How sweet of you." She wrinkled her brow thoughtfully. "Let me think—how often have I assisted at a friend's bridal? Once—twice? What's the saying—'Three times a bridesmaid, never a bride!' Can I bear the fate? But when's the great day?"

"We haven't fixed a date, but somewhere around three weeks hence," said Blair.

"From the hospital, of course?" asked Lorna. And as Jean shook her head: "No?"

"We're being married down here," said Blair. "Less fuss."

"You *are* extraordinary people!" laughed Lorna. "You can't really mean to do it in this hole-in-the-corner spot. Don't let him do you out of your wedding, Jean—half the hospital will want to be there."

"That's it," said Blair. "And why we are keeping the date quiet."

"Heavens! I can't cope!" Lorna shrugged. "But it's your wedding. May I let you know about my part in it, in a day or two?"

"Of course," Jean agreed, relieved by the conviction that her offer would be refused.

And Lorna was thinking: It was maddening enough to have to listen to Aunt Harriet discussing arrangements for the wedding which she, Lorna, would have done anything in her power to prevent, without having to take a prominent part in it.

An hour later, when she drove off with Blair, who could hardly refuse to take her the few miles back to her friends, she was all smiles and warmth, and declaring that weddings were the greatest fun, and it was "*sweet* of Jean to want her to assist".

While, watching the car disappearing, Jean knew that the other girl's unexpected appearance had thrown a shadow over her week-end. She knew so well that Lorna disliked her and, being no fool, also knew why.

Chapter 12

I

After that visit to Blair's home the days sped by so rapidly that when she realised another week had actually gone, Jean could hardly believe it. Cinderella ward was going through one of its most crowded periods, and as usual at that kind of time — as Lorna grumbled — there was a shortage of staff. Two of the student nurses, having both caught a throat infection, were temporarily out of action.

By now Jean's staff knew that she was leaving, and the reason was no longer a secret to them.

"If this goes on when there is a new Sister-in-Charge, I shall go bonkers!" Sally Blaker told Jean. "I'm sure things will never be the same again when you have gone. Temple says she's going to take up a job in that new nursing home in Cavendish Square. Not that — " She stopped, biting her lip, remembering that Lorna would be a connection by marriage of Sister's. "I hate change," she added hurriedly. "In spite of any ups and downs, we've been just one happy family on Cinderella. I can't believe we shall only have you for another week. And I hear there's an entire stranger coming in your place — quite new to the hospital."

"Matron says Sisters are running short," said Jean. "But I gather my successor is a St. Catherine's nurse — or was. She trained here, and she's been at a big hospital in the Midlands."

But Blaker, who thought the world of Jean, and was the only person whom the latter had ever allowed herself to be really friendly with, was not to be comforted.

This conversation took place in Sister's office, and when Sally had gone, Jean sat staring thoughtfully before her. Was it possible that in just another week all this would be behind her for ever, and she would be beginning yet another new life?

As soon as she left the hospital she would go straight down to Polsford, but meanwhile it had been arranged that she and Blair would spend the coming Sunday at Arleigh Hall. Meanwhile, Lorna had finally decided that she would not risk the superstitious belief about being a bridesmaid for a third time.

But "Uncle Leo" — Colonel Temple, who was Mrs. Marston's only brother, was to give Jean away, while Mrs. Marston had got her wish about the wedding dress. She had come up to London and taken Jean to order it, coaxing the famous couturier to do a rush job, and it was being sent down into the country to await its wearer. But though the whole hospital knew that Sister Campbell was leaving to marry Mr. Marston, where and when the ceremony was to take place still seemed vague. It was only afterwards Jean realised why she had been so secretive; somewhere inside her there had been a growing doubt of her happiness lasting.

Rousing herself from the reverie into which she had fallen, she glanced down with a half sigh at her wrist-watch.

Another hour and she would be free; usually that knowledge brought with it a quickened sense of happy expectation, because she would be spending at least part of the evening with Blair. As a rule they dined together, or if he could not get away until later she waited for him at his flat, or met him somewhere. But she was not looking forward to this evening as much as usual.

Ever since that Sunday in Suffolk Lorna had shown every desire to get more friendly with her, and Jean felt guilty because she could not respond as warmly as she felt she ought to, but she could rid herself of the feeling that Nurse Temple was completely insincere.

While Jean was on holiday, Lorna had exchanged her quarters in the nurses' hostel for a furnished flat of her own, and was now ensconced in her new home, which was quite some way from the hospital. As she had a very comfortable private income and ran her own car, the journey between home and work did not worry her. She had been pressing Jean and Blair to have dinner with her, and though they had managed to avoid that, they had finally felt forced to accept an invitation to have drinks at her flat, and the occasion had been arranged for that evening. But Blair did not expect to be free until much later, so it was decided that he would join the two girls as soon as he could get away.

It had been Lorna's free afternoon, and as no amount of staff shortage would ever induce that young woman to put herself out by remaining on duty when she could avoid it, she had taken her leave with blithe disregard for any inconvenience that it might cause.

Certainly Cinderella's staff nurse would not be too badly missed when she went to her new job, Jean decided. It was no use pretending—she was sure that she could never get really friendly with Blair's cousin; all the time they had been on Cinderella together Lorna had shown no sign of wanting to cultivate her acquaintance, and if she was doing it now, it was because she thought it would please Blair. Nevertheless, Jean felt, it was up to herself to try to meet the other girl as near half way as possible.

When, an hour later, she pressed the bell beside the white painted door of Lorna's new home, she was hoping Blair would not be kept too long. There was a pause before Lorna opened the door herself, and held out both hands in welcome.

"There you are! I'm so glad you are such a blessedly punctual person," she greeted, drawing her visitor inside. "Only that makes it just too bad that you should arrive too late to have a word with your young man."

"With Blair?" asked Jean, trying not to sound apprehensive, but hoping desperately he had not rung to say he could not come.

"It's all right, darling," assured Lorna. "He only rang to say he might be a bit later than he expected, and we were to keep sober until he arrived." She did not explain that she had been speaking to Blair when she heard Jean's ring, and had deliberately not told him to hold on. "Anyhow," she added, "we can have a nice cosy gossip before he arrives. Sit there, Jean, and relax. I suppose this afternoon has been no less complicated than usual?"

"Fairly hectic," Jean answered, taking the chair her hostess indicated.

"*Darling*, won't you be grateful to finish with it all?" asked Lorna. She had a habit of addressing everyone as "darling", and Jean could not help the insincerity jarring on her.

"No, I've loved every bit of it," she replied.

Fetching a box of cigarettes, Lorna regarded her from under raised brows. "Of course, you're so perfectly dedicated. Not like me who—how can I put it?—well, couldn't carry on unless I got away from it all sometimes."

"You seem to have managed that very well here." Jean glanced round the exotic décor of the room, with its very modern chairs and general air of luxurious comfort in the Scandinavian style, and then back to her companion who could not possibly have looked more unlike the neatly uniformed staff nurse on Cinderella. Lorna was wearing a peacock blue trouser suit, tightly fitting enough to show every line of her remarkably beautiful body. Sally Blaker had once said: "I don't know how Temple manages it, but she always seems to give the impression that she hasn't anything on under her uniform!"

This evening, with her red gold hair looking as though it had just been restyled, and against the background of the cyclamen, black, and silver room, Jean found it more impossible than ever to understand why the other girl had chosen nursing as a profession.

"Cigarette?" Lorna held out the box, and as Jean helped herself: "What are you thinking of so disapprovingly?"

"I wasn't—I mean—Honestly, Lorna, what made you become a nurse?" Jean blurted out.

Lorna shrugged. "Well—believe it or not, I've got a scientific mind. I like to find out how the wheels go round—I ought really to have gone in for psychiatry."

A scientific mind! Yes, thought Jean. But is it a human

one? She was very efficient, but she had never really seemed to give love or understanding to her small patients, and that was why it had not been possible to like her.

"Anyway, it was a toss-up between nursing and the stage. 'Science' won!" Lorna told her.

But why St. Catherine's, of all hospitals? I'm glad she's leaving! thought Jean. Aloud she asked: "Do you think you will like your new job?"

"Yes; it will be such a complete change." Lorna lowered herself gracefully into a chair. "It would be waste, I suppose, to chuck nursing now. This place I'm going to is run by Sir Robert Conyers-Evans — it's the last word in luxury. I expect I shall have some horrible rich old women to nurse, but I'll get a lot more time to myself, and not so much red tape." There was no need to explain that she hoped for some "very rich" male patients, and to come into contact with some equally rich doctors, who were bound to be interested in a beautiful and attractive nurse! Lorna was a realist to her finger-tips; frustrated though she was over Blair, she still intended to make the kind of marriage that appealed to her. Sir Robert Conyers-Evans was a very successful man and, at forty, still a bachelor.

After a slight pause she said suddenly: "You know, Jean, I do think you're marvellous the way you've let Blair have all his own way about your wedding. I mean, having it down at Polsford, being married from Arleigh Hall and keeping it all so frightfully hush-hush. It wouldn't do for me! After all, it's about the best opportunity in a girl's life to cut a real dash and show people how marvellous she can look. And you really will make a very decorative bride."

Jean's laugh was frankly amused. "So long as Blair thinks so, that will be all I care about — as far as the decoration goes," she replied. "And as for giving in to him — we're two minds with but a single thought in that direction. I want a quiet wedding as much as he does."

"Oh, well, everyone to their own taste." Lorna shrugged; then after another pause: "But wouldn't you like some of your own friends in Scotland to have come down for it? You must have relatives?" She finished on a note of enquiry.

Jean hesitated, fully aware of the curiosity in the other's eyes. It was not the first time that Lorna, by gentle probing, had obviously sought to get her to talk about herself.

"I have no family," she admitted quietly. "And as far as friends — well, it's a long time since I was up north, and one — loses touch."

"No one of your own at all! Poor Jean, you must have been awfully lonely! Do you know," Lorna sat forward, the warmth in her voice finding no reflection in her aquamarine eyes, "I've often thought you were a real lone wolf; I mean, you don't make friends easily, do you?"

"Not very easily, perhaps."

"How lovely that you'll have Blair!"

"Yes, it is —" At that moment the front door bell interrupted any further cross-examination.

"Talk of angels! That must be Blair." Lorna rose quickly. Outside in the small hallway her smile faded and her brows drew together. She had hoped to find out more, even at the risk of being thought inquisitive — but heavens! How difficult Jean was to *get* at!

She was smiling again when she opened the front door.

"Blair — *darling!* Go right in while I collect ice for the drinks," she greeted.

He needed no urge to obey her, and turning towards the kitchenette, she heard him say: "Hello, sweetheart. I thought I was never going to get away."

When she rejoined her guests, Blair was standing beside his fiancée, and seeing them together, a shaft of angry jealousy shot through her.

"Mix the drinks, Blair," she requested, smiling at him. "I'm sure Jean needs one, and I'm quite ready for sustenance." She glanced at her wrist-watch. "It's long past opening time, and this is a sort of housewarming, you know — you're the first people I've had here. I think it's absolutely low of you not to have said you'd stay to dinner. I suppose, my coz., you thought me incapable of cooking a decent meal."

"You're hardly attired for domesticity!" he retorted with cousinly frankness.

"Rubbish! I can cook in anything from a bikini to — Oh, anything at all!" she retorted. "And I assure you, I *can* cook."

He raised his brows. "I'll take your word for it."

"Well, come along and mix those drinks — perhaps you'll feel less sceptical when you've had one," she told him.

Watching her directing Blair, Jean was fully aware of the air of possession which had always characterised Lorna's manner towards him, but without feeling a pang.

When they were all settled again, and in possession of their glasses, Lorna asked: "Well, Mr. Marston, what do you think of my new quarters?"

He looked round critically. "Very exotic. And quite unlike the home life of our dear hospital!"

Jean laughed spontaneously. "You ought to ask Matron to tea, Lorna," she said.

"That would be the day, wouldn't it! But seriously," Lorna urged, "don't you think I was clever as well as lucky, to get this place? Every other tenant in the house is a doctor, two of them women, and if I hadn't known someone who pulled strings for me — "

"My dear Lorna, don't you always manage to get what you want?" he asked amusedly. "By fair means or foul!"

Her face set. "Not always!" And then hastily covering the sudden bitterness: "Jean, will you please teach your young man to be kinder to his cousin — he's in a hateful mood."

"He's only teasing," soothed Jean. "You ought to be used to him. It's a lovely flat, anyway."

"Tell me," urged Lorna, "are you two going down to The Hall this week-end? If so, I'd better warn you that I've invited myself. Auntie says Annette will still be there."

"We shall only get down for the day, I'm afraid," Blair answered. "Probably not until lunch time, and we'll have to leave after dinner. I'm operating early on Monday, and Jean will have to be on duty. By the way, sweetheart," he added, "I saw that rather randy old friend of yours on my way here — what's his name? McNairn?"

"Neil McNairn!" Taken aback Jean could not keep

the dismay from her tone. She flushed, biting her lip, aware of her hostess's instant interest.

"Yes, didn't you know he was around?" asked Blair.

"No." Her voice was steady now, and if she was paler than usual, Blair was not the person who noticed.

He laughed. "I wondered if he'd called on you again. If he does, for heaven's sake don't ask him to see you married."

She shook her head. "He's—not likely to come. Where did you see him?"

"Matter of fact, he nearly walked under my car. But he didn't recognise me."

"Don't tell me Jean has a randy boy friend!" laughed Lorna. "Who is he, Jean—a bit of your dark past?"

"Not exactly." How many times in her career, and how often would she still have to be, grateful for the training which had taught such rigid self-control—though it had nearly deserted her just now. For somehow, believing that he really had gone back north, a reminder of the man who was so closely connected with all she wanted to forget (those things which he himself had urged her to forget) had come as an unpleasant shock. She could not help wondering why he was still in London; if by some evil chance he was in need of help again and would contact her.

"By the way, Blair," she said quickly, "Annette telephoned me this morning. She's spending Saturday night in town, and she would like us to take her down to your mother's on Sunday."

Neil McNairn was not mentioned again, and though he remained a little disquietingly in her mind, when the end of the week came without any sign from him, she decided that he evidently had no intention of calling on her. Whatever he might be doing in London, it appeared that he was going to keep the promise he had made to her, and not attempt to see her again.

II

On that particular Saturday evening Lorna was booked to have dinner with the R.M.O. of St. Catherine's—a gay and extremely attractive young man on whom she occasionally bestowed her company.

Spending a few pleasant hours with him, she thought, as she had often done before, what a pity it was that Ned Easterby hadn't more money, and more ambition. However, it was a not unsatisfactory *affaire pour passer le temps*, and their meetings soothed, if only briefly, the sense of angry frustration from which she was suffering.

They dined at a quiet restaurant near the hospital, but Dr. Easterby was obliged to be back on duty by nine-thirty. Lorna's car was being overhauled, and after bidding her host good night, she decided to stroll westward, until she felt inclined to hail a taxi to take her home.

She had not seen Blair since he and Jean had had drinks with her, and the only words they had exchanged had been of business-like brevity. But it was Jean who was occupying her mind most strongly, while she made her leisurely way along the pavements.

Jean, who in such a disturbingly short time would be married to Blair. It was maddening to be forced to stand by and see the thing she would have given so much to prevent happen. Heaven knew, she thought bitterly, she had never liked Jean! But since Jean's engagement to her cousin, the dislike had grown into an almost pathological hatred. Selfish and acquisitive to the core, the frustration of having her cherished plans ruined maddened her. Were there no means of convincing Blair of the utter unsuitability of the marriage he contemplated?

And that everybody — but everybody — should be so besotted with the so-and-so, made it more stupid. When she had just hinted to Annette that it was a pity Blair had not chosen someone with a more distinct social background, Annette had retorted: "Don't be such a crashing snob, Lorna! He couldn't have chosen anyone sweeter. You say she's reticent about her family — what nonsense! Do you really expect her to produce a pedigree?"

"Of course not!" Lorna had protested. "But I have a certain amount of family pride, and if he were my brother I should want to be sure his wife would not produce some impossible-to-know relative at an awkward moment." At which Annette hooted derisively. An exchange which did not improve an already cool relationship between the cousins.

But that did not alter Lorna's attitude in this, to her, vital matter.

If Jean had nothing that she wanted to hide, why could she not be more frank about herself? Why had she become such an adept at avoiding direct answers to direct questions? Why, in all these years at St. Catherine's had she never made one intimate friend? Why—Oh, why a hundred things! thought Lorna impatiently. Heaven knew, she had done her utmost during these last weeks to get on really intimate terms with Jean. But it was like coming up against a stone wall; there must be something behind that wall, or it would not have been so carefully built and preserved.

There was a petty, spiteful streak in Lorna's nature, which would have found the greatest pleasure in simply discovering anything, however innocent, that it would hurt Jean's pride to have her know.

"Excuse me. Could you tell me where Rowanton Mansions is?"

Lorna started, dragged back from her thoughts to consciousness of her surroundings, and found herself looking into the rather anxious face of the enquirer, a grey-haired woman with a strong foreign accent. "I think I lose myself," the stranger said ruefully. "I was told it was near the children's 'ospital."

"Yes, it's somewhere round here. Why—there it is!" Lorna pointed to the building outside which they had both stopped.

"Oh, how foolish! Thank you so much."

"Not at all."

The stranger hurried up the short flight of steps leading to the block of flats, and disappeared inside. Lorna was about to walk on when she stopped abruptly, again looking back at the building.

Rowanton Mansions? Why was the name familiar?

Then she remembered. Of course—that was where Jean lived.

She hesitated for a moment. Then: "Why not?" she asked herself. However unwelcome her visit might be, it would be—interesting to see Sister Campbell in her own surroundings, and what more natural—since she was passing!—than to obey a sudden impulse and call in.

That was another thing, now she came to think of it. "Sister" never seemed to ask any of the staff to visit her for a drink, or even the odd cup of tea or coffee. Something her predecessor had often done. Well, she was going to have a visitor now!

Rowanton Mansions was not a new building; it had been built, in fact, before the last war—one of those blocks of semi-service flatlets that always have a slightly institutional suggestion about them, but still fail to be as intimidating as the horrible new concrete towers that are ruining London's skyline.

An old hall porter, intent on checking the football results in his copy of an evening paper, looked up when she spoke to him.

"Miss Campbell? The nurse? Fourth floor, turn left when you get out of the lift. Number 140." No, he hadn't seen her go out, but he had only been on duty for the last half hour.

Lorna took herself up in the rather noisy lift, and leaving it on the fourth floor, had no difficulty in finding the number she sought.

She had pressed the bell beside the front door before she noticed the man who was leaning against the wall in the shadows near it.

Quick to observe, her brief glance at him noted his shabbiness. He and she were the only sign of life in the long passage between rows of tightly shut doors, and she wondered what he was doing so obviously loitering, and if the porter knew he was there.

Then as she reached a finger towards the bell again, the man straightened, and turning towards her, spoke.

"I'm afraid there's no one in. I've rung three times, but

no luck." The voice, considering the appearance of its owner, was unexpectedly cultured.

As Lorna looked round, he stared back at her from slightly prominent, bloodshot eyes. "I — was — waiting," he explained. "Because I've rather particular bus — business. Maybe you're expected, and Jea — she'll be back to meet you."

It did not need the over-careful intonation, or the strong smell of spirits that reached her, for Lorna to place his type at sight. But it was the slight suggestion of a Scottish accent that was probably not there when he was sober — which he was obviously not at present — that quickened her interest.

She gave him a friendly smile. "I am afraid I only looked in on chance. Were you waiting for Jean Campbell?"

"Yes, I was." He swayed slightly. "Waiting for Jeannie."

"I see. Perhaps I could give her a message for you in the morning. She and I work together at the hospital — "

"Is that so? But 'fraid you can't help. I'll just have to go on waiting until she comes."

Here was an odd acquaintance for the so very exclusive Sister Campbell! Obviously a fellow countryman, and —

Then with startling suddenness Lorna remembered Blair's half laughing, half disapproving remark to Jean when they had been with her the other evening.

"*I saw your randy boy friend.*" And Jean's startled: "*Neil McNairn?*"

The kind of name one would remember. And as Jean could hardly have a collection of "randy" boy friends, this was intriguing.

Lorna looked more closely at her companion. Hardly the type of gentleman Blair would appreciate calling on his fiancée. Lorna flashed another of her charming smiles at him, determined to pursue this chance acquaintance.

"Is it Mr. McNairn?" she asked. "I've heard Jean speak of you. She's marrying my cousin, you know."

He looked surprised. If his mind had been clearer, the surprise would have been more distinct, but he would most certainly not have pursued the subject until he had mentioned this meeting to Jean. Indeed, if he had been strictly sober he would not have been here at all. But though as far as appearances went — for his first slightly slurred speech advertised that he was on the brink of reaching "one over the eight" — he had been drinking quite heavily, and was now at the stage when another whisky, and then another and another, seemed not only desirable but absolutely necessary. He was too broke to buy himself even one! But here was an extremely good looking young woman who seemed inclined to be sympathetic, and his immediate reaction was to confide in her.

"So Jeannie told you about ol' Neil," he said. "Best and — oldest friend she has. She should be here to help me now. I'm," in his turn he flashed a suddenly charming smile, "I'm in — the devil of a hole."

"Are you? How tiresome for you."

He nodded. "Masterly understatement, dear lady. Had — had my pocket picked. Wallet gone." He snapped his fingers. "Must have happened on the train. I was depending on finding Jeannie. However, I'll just have to be waiting here to borrow the price of a night's lodging. Forgive these sordid revelations."

"But how awful for you!" Lorna's heart was beating quickly. Could this be the chance in a million for which she had never dared hope? Who was this broken down wreck who claimed to be Jean's oldest friend? She understood now that Blair's description of him had been a joke.

"How stupid I am!" she exclaimed. "Of course — I'd quite forgotten. Jean won't be back until late, and then she won't be alone. Anyhow, you can't wait here indefinitely. Perhaps — please don't be offended, I could help?"

"My dear girl — young — lady — "

"I tell you what," she interrupted. "I am — just going to get something to eat. Perhaps you would care to come along with me. We could have a drink and a snack, and then perhaps you could ring Jean and find out if she's back. If not, as you're such an old friend, I'm sure she would like me to help."

"But this is munificent kindness! Hardly like to take

advantage." McNairn straightened. His pride had vanished long ago, and yet just for a moment the idea of sponging on a strange woman was on the point of worrying all that was left of the gentleman in him. Seeing his hesitation, with a growing anxiety not to let him go, Lorna said smilingly:

"Don't be silly! Jean would never forgive me if I left you stranded. Do let's go."

But if by some unlucky chance they met Jean before she got him out of the building, she could not help wondering exactly how she would manage the situation!

Chapter 13

I

Blair had arranged to call for Jean on Sunday morning, and picking up Annette first, they left London before ten o'clock.

Jean did not hear anything of Neil McNairn that night, and having almost forgotten him, she had slept soundly.

But while she waited for Blair to arrive, she had been wishing she could have found some excuse to avoid going down to Arleigh Hall this week-end. She had looked forward to spending the day with Mrs. Marston until she learned that Lorna was going to join the family party; somehow that knowledge had the power to spoil the day before it began.

But when they arrived there was no sign of Lorna, and Mrs. Marston said that her niece had telephoned, saying she would not be arriving until tea-time.

As they entered the house Annette came running down-stairs to greet them, and turning to Jean told her:

"My dear, The Dress has arrived! I put the box up in the Blue Room. I could hardly stop myself from unpacking it; do come and show it to me," she continued gaily: "I was not half so excited over my own wedding dress, was I, Mummy?"

But her mother only laughed, saying, "Run along, you two. Blair will stay with me."

"He certainly will. You are not in on this act—yet," Annette told her brother.

The Blue Room was the one Jean had occupied on that first week-end. As they entered it now the first thing she saw was the big silvered dress box reposing on the bed. She had seen her wedding dress twice already—the first time Mrs. Marston had been with her, but on the second occasion she had gone alone. And in one of the couturier's grey and gold salons, had watched a lovely model who was wearing it, parading for her benefit. But somehow she had not been able quite to believe that the lovely gown was meant for her; that in a short while she would actually walk down the aisle in it—while Blair waited for her, to take the vows that would bind them together for ever.

While she undid the silver cords fastening the box, Annette watched.

"Mummy is already calling this room yours," she said. "She means you and Blair to occupy it whenever you come to stay, after you are married."

"How dear of her." Jean felt a little catch in her throat. "That makes me feel as if I really belonged."

"So you do," Annette told her. "I couldn't welcome anyone Blair had chosen, more gladly. I can't tell you how relieved I was when I met you! You see, Blair and I, being the only ones, still remained pretty close, even after I married. I've dreaded him getting someone whom I might hate!" she confessed frankly. "I didn't really believe Lorna would ever succeed in getting him, but I had a tiny fear that if she was persevering enough, and he suddenly decided that it really was time he married, her persistence might win. Though bless his heart, I'm sure he never realised what she was after. Did you?"

"I—wondered," Jean admitted.

"Surely you could not have been so blind, that you didn't see what was going on under your nose?" asked Annette. "I just could not have borne it if she *had* got him. I really would have thought up something drastic!"

Jean made no comment. Her hands were not quite steady, and her heart was racing while she lifted the dress from its wrappings. And a lovely thing it was—a frock of soft clinging ivory satin, almost entirely simple in its straight slenderness, long sleeved and with a cowl neckline.

"Oh, grand!" Annette approved. "The great man has

surpassed himself! It's so completely you. No frills, and lots of dignity."

"Good grief! What do you make me sound like?" Jean laughed.

"A bit of a nun, but a very human one. My blue will look lovely against that. But you must have something blue too. You've got the something 'borrowed' in Mummy's wedding veil. I wore that. They did my wedding dress too, you know. Aren't those boxes, specially for weddings, charming? He sends bridesmaids' regalias packed in whatever colour has been chosen. Mine were blush pink, ducky— Lorna was livid! Pink doesn't really suit her," Annette finished with delicate malice.

Jean laid the dress across the day bed and as Annette arranged the train, which was embroidered with silver lilies, Mrs. Marston came into the room.

Jean ran to her impulsively. "It's lovely!" she cried. "I can't thank you enough. I shall keep it for ever."

"My dear child!" Blair's mother kissed her and, hands on her shoulders, held her, looking up into her face. "Be good to him, Jean!"

"Indeed I will—"

Annette, still busy with her arrangements, said: "I'll put it away for you later. Leave it there for the time. There's the gong—"

"And your starving young man waiting for his lunch, Jean!" said Mrs. Marston.

Jean was the last to leave the room. She paused for a moment to look back. It was only afterwards she realised her last glimpse of her wedding dress had been through the sudden tears that dimmed her eyes. The next moment she shut the door and followed the others.

Blair was waiting at the bottom of the stairs, and seeing him the fearful half doubt, which had suddenly stirred, was stillborn. He belonged to tomorrow—all those tomorrows she would share with him, while—those other things belonged to yesterday.

And nothing could call back yesterday.

After lunch Jean and Blair wandered through the woods behind the house. The lovely green silence of high summer lay all about them; strolling along the paths beneath the trees they seemed to have the whole world to themselves. Presently they sat down on a fallen tree trunk, and knocking the ashes from his pipe, Blair put an arm about his companion, drawing her against him.

"In one more week, my darling," he said, half humorously, "you will be stuck with me for the rest of my life. How daunting do you find that idea?"

"I find it most attractive," she told him.

"I still feel rather guilty!" he observed.

"Guilty? You!" She was oddly startled.

He laughed. "Yes. Every time I go into Cinderella, I shall see those rows of little beds reproaching me for stealing you away. Also, I shall miss 'Sister'. Very illogical of me! I can't eat my cake and have it. But you have spoilt me. Old Maynard-Phillips was telling me yesterday that I ought to be shot for robbing the hospital of one of the best nursing Sisters ever born."

"What nonsense!" Jean exclaimed. "There will be another, equally good." But she wondered, rather apprehensively, if anyone else would feel quite the deep love for her ward that had filled her from the beginning.

Blair gave her an intent look. "You're going to miss your work, my sweet—as much as it will miss you."

"Of course I shall miss it. I shall miss the children, and the sense of being necessary—"

"You certainly needn't miss that! You will be more necessary than you have ever been in your life. And I am a complete fraud," he confessed. "I am not really in the least ashamed of my piratical behaviour. Everything sensible and—otherwise—in me, tells me how right I am to carry you off! Other people have had quite enough of you—you belong to me now."

"I know that." She lifted her lips to meet his, and for a long moment he held her close, whispering unsteadily:

"What should I have done if I had never found you, my darling?" And then holding her a little away from him: "I wonder if you ever guess how empty my life would be without you? How I need you."

Looking into his eyes she did realise it, and once again found every reason for dedicating the rest of her own life to making a success of the one they would soon begin together.

She was filled with a deep new kind of happiness when, half an hour later, they returned to the house.

The tea table was spread under the cedar tree on the lawn, and seeing the group of people about it, Blair exclaimed softly: "Visitors! Blast!"

She shook her head at him. "You mustn't be anti-social. It's a terrible trait in a doctor's character. Come along and do be polite, darling." She had recognised Sir James and Lady Drummond at once, but there were three other guests who had risen and were inspecting the wide herbaceous border a little distance away. They turned and came back as Jean and Blair drew nearer and, her smile fading, Jean saw that one of them was Lorna.

"Hello, you two!" Lorna called. "Here I am again! What heavenly weather you've got for me. It was pouring when I left town." And when, having greeted Sir James and his wife, Jean took the chair Mrs. Marston beckoned her to: "Blair, your young woman is getting sunburnt."

"Dreadful, isn't it?" said Jean. "I burn as dark as a gypsy whenever the sun comes out."

"Being a blonde, I'm horribly inclined to turn pink—so I take good care," said Lorna, who was wearing a vastly becoming broad-brimmed hat. "By the way, you don't know Jean Campbell, do you, Cynthia—Mrs. Egerton, Jean—Mr. Egerton—Sister Campbell is Blair's fiancée."

Ian Egerton, a stocky, fair man, gave his new acquaintance a frankly approving glance. "Lucky Blair! How do you do, Miss Campbell."

"No, we haven't met, but I've heard about you," said his wife, more curiosity than approval in her stare. "Mr.

137

Marston, I haven't had a chance to congratulate you. Both of you, please, take it for granted."

"Thank you." Blair, who had been greeting his mother's other two guests, said: "How are you, Ian. No need to ask you, Cynthia, though no doubt you're still burning the candle till it melts."

"Miss Campbell, could you make him be polite to me?" Mrs. Egerton asked. "He has known me too long to cultivate a bedside manner." Then without waiting for a reply she told Blair: "We're all madly thrilled over this wedding."

"Indeed, yes," said Lady Drummond. "You will have the whole W.I. turning out as an adoring bodyguard, Blair. There was a heated argument among the older members after they heard of your engagement, as to which of them remembered you longest."

Blair laughed. "I refuse to believe the oldest inhabitant nursed me, or gazed upon me when I was in my pram."

"Everyone will think it so sweet that you are going to be married down here," Lady Drummond told him. "And you too, Miss Campbell. We were afraid you were going for a big London affair."

While tea progressed the baronet discussed local affairs with Mrs. Marston, but his wife proved less impersonal, and asked frankly:

"You are — or were — nursing at St. Catherine's, were you not?"

Jean nodded. "Yes, I have been there for some years."

"How very interesting. One of my husband's sisters is a nurse — in Newcastle." She mentioned the name of the hospital, and after an imperceptible hesitation Jean told her:

"I trained there."

"Really? Then I wonder if you met. Margaret has been there for four years now, and has just been made a Sister — Margaret Langley."

"No. She would be after my time." Jean wished the conversation would take another turn. Lady Drummond, who was very English County, and as important as her husband in the neighbourhood, was clearly out to find out all she could about Blair's choice, and although there was no reason why Jean should not speak of her former hospital, she wondered how inquisitive this rather arrogant lady was likely to prove.

"Isn't that interesting?" She turned to her husband. "Miss—or ought I to say 'Sister' Campbell trained at St. Cuthbert's where Meg is. And you're Scottish, aren't you?" she asked Jean.

"Yes." Jean was suddenly aware Lorna was watching her closely.

Her ladyship's cross-examination continued. "Would you be any relation to the Campbells of Ardloch?"

"No. My father came from farther north," said Jean quietly.

Sir James said genially: "Too bad if I cannot claim kinship. But I still approve of Blair's choice of a Scottish lassie to keep him in good order!"

"Talking of Scotland," said Lorna. "You will know the answer to this, Sir James. What does a verdict of 'non proven' mean?"

Jean felt herself stiffen. All at once the sunlit gardens darkened, as though a menacing shadow had fallen across them. Looking down at her clasped hands she was relieved to see how steady they were; but above the loud beating of her heart Sir James's voice sounded strangely muffled, when he replied:

"Well now, that's something that doesn't happen on this side of the border—"

"But what does it mean?" Lorna persisted. "I do realise that it is something peculiar to Scottish law, but I can't quite make out whether it means that a jury disagrees, if the person they decide not to convict goes out into the world without a stain on their character, or what? Until the other day I thought there couldn't be anything but a verdict of 'guilty', in a criminal trial."

Sir James smiled indulgently. "I hope you are not expecting me to give a lecture on criminal proceedings, although before I married and—emigrated!—I trained for the

Scottish Bar." He chuckled, glancing at his wife. Then more seriously: "But to try to answer your question, Lorna. Well, in England, if there is not sufficient evidence, the case breaks down, doesn't it?"

"Ye-es. I suppose so. I'm an awful dunce about these things." Lorna was at her most feminine as she flashed an uncertain smile at the old gentleman. "Is that the same as 'non proven'?"

"In a way. I don't suppose you ever heard of the famous case in Victorian times, when a young woman named Madeline Smith was tried for poisoning her lover? The verdict then was 'non proven', though I doubt very much if she would have got away with it in England."

"I gather that was one of the most sensational legal cases in history," said Blair.

"It was," agreed Sir James.

"Well, I should think the one I have in mind was really much the same," said Lorna. "And it only happened about seven years ago. Perhaps you will remember it, Sir James? The girl in the case was a Jean Stewart—"

Sir James shook his head. "I don't recollect it. I doubt if I would have known about it. Seven years since, I had retired from practice."

"If it was seven years ago," his wife put in, "we were in South Africa. I don't remember seeing anything about a Scottish murder case—anyhow, we were on safari, and did not see a paper for weeks."

"For some reason or other the case seems to have got crowded out of the English newspapers," Lorna told her. "I think you must have heard about it, Jean." Flicking the ash from her cigarette, she looked towards Jean, her eyes hard. "It happened in Edinburgh, and caused an enormous sensation there, because so many people thought the verdict should have been 'guilty', and that only a superlatively clever counsel got the girl off, though he couldn't get an outright 'not guilty' verdict." She was looking at Blair now. "I was told this story by—someone I met the other night. The conversation turned on famous trials, and this man mentioned the Jean Stewart case—sorry, Jean, I'm afraid the heroine had your first name, and she was not at all a nice young woman."

"Jean is hardly an uncommon name in Scotland," said Blair coldly.

"I know; but I think that is one Jean who ought not to be running about the world. I'm longing to hear Sir James agree with me." Lorna looked towards him, then back at Jean, and for a moment held the other girl's eyes.

There was no mistaking the malice and open challenge in her look. But though Jean knew she was watching the whole lovely fabric of her dream being destroyed, she was determined her tormentor should not see her blench. She had always known Lorna disliked her, and now at last all pretence was done away with, and she was facing an open enemy.

"I hope I'm not being a bore," Lorna said, all the feline in her loving her cat and mouse game.

"You're not boring *me*," Cynthia Egerton told her. "I'm a thriller fan, and this sounds right up my street. Do go on."

"O.K. Here goes." Lorna leant back, crossing her slender knees.

"The Cardine murder case—chapter one: It appears that this Jean Stewart lass was a daughter of the manse, as I gather they describe a minister's daughter in Scotland—from some remote island or other. When she was just over sixteen her father died, and as there was little or no money Jean had to earn her living. There was not much scope on the island, and an old friend of her father's (not a minister), who lived in Edinburgh, offered to pay for a course of secretarial training. I can guess she seized on the idea of escaping to the capital (I'm sorry, but to make things clear, I may sound a bit long winded)." She avoided her aunt's eyes, though she was well aware that Mrs. Marston disapproved of her choice of subject. But she, Lorna, had taken a day off on the plea of illness, and spent it among old newspaper files in the British Museum Newspaper department out at Collingdale?

"Well?" Sir James prompted.

"Well," she gave him her attention. "Jean Stewart did her training, and managed somehow to get a job as secretary to a man called Ronald Cardine, who had written a good bit for the stage and television, and was considered rather *the* coming playwright. He was all mixed up with a bohemian, decidedly rapid set — writers, actors, and artists, a circle of whom Cardine was the leading light. Apart from his cleverness — it seems he was really brilliant — he was a decidedly bad lad, with a very off reputation where the ladies were concerned; he was very handsome and the kind of personality to attract an adventurous young woman who was at an impressionable age. She admitted that she admired and thought a great deal of her employer, though when she was put in the witness box later she only admitted to 'hero-worship', and said 'innocently' she had not believed a word when she was warned about him.

"The story — her story — was that he was working on a new play. He had finished, and asked her to work very late one night. She swore that he had never previously made a pass at her, and that nothing had ever surprised or frightened her more than when he proceeded to do just that — plus!

"They had been working until well after midnight, and she was just going home when he suddenly got fresh. She had a struggle with him, and locked herself in another room, because 'she was scared he would stop her if she tried the front door'! It appears that on that night a man — an actor — who lived in the flat underneath Cardine's, had been out until late. It was an old-fashioned block, let out in offices below and with no lift. It was nearly one o'clock when he — the actor — let himself in, and he was climbing the stairs when Jean Stewart came hurrying down them.

"He knew her slightly, and realising she was upset, tried to stop her, but she brushed past him and rushed out of the building. Deciding it was not his business and thinking that she had had a row with 'the boy friend', he shrugged the incident off.

"The flat opposite Cardine's was occupied by another bachelor — a barrister. Both were at the top of the building.

142

The barrister man had been dining with some friends. After dinner they played cards far into the night, and it was past four o'clock when he — this other neighbour of the writer's — arrived home. When he reached the landing he saw that the door of Cardine's place was open. There had been a series of burglaries around that time, and as he didn't hear anyone moving, it seems that his legal mind became suspicious, and instead of letting himself into his own flat, he went across and called his neighbour's name. There was no reply; no sign of anyone being awake; no light in the hall, but one showing under the sitting-room door. He knocked at it, and when no one answered his suspicion that there was something wrong increased. He went into the room, and found Cardine lying face downwards on the carpet. He had been shot in the back.

"Naturally, knowing all the right procedure, this man — left everything untouched and rang the police. It turned out that the shot had been fired at close enough range to smother the report. The police could find no sign of a weapon, and when it came to finger-prints the only ones were on the handle of the room door (that room led off the one where the dead man was found), and they belonged to both the dead man and his secretary. There were signs of a struggle. A chair had been overturned, and there was a heavy paper-weight which could have been thrown. As the flat below had been empty until the man who met Jean Stewart on the stairs returned, no one had heard a thing. The actor told the police about the encounter on the stairs, and it seemed clear that Cardine's secretary had been the only person with him that night. When the police went to interview her, she was very hastily packing, with, she admitted, the intention of leaving Edinburgh that night, though she would not say where she intended to go."

"So the girl was arrested," said Sir James. "Naturally. It seems simple enough."

"It certainly does," agreed Lorna. "Nevertheless, the girl got off. For some philanthropic reason or other, the barrister — or advocate — man who found the body, and who didn't seem to be very fond of Mr. Cardine, decided to defend the girl. He was evidently a brilliant man, and — well, he got, perhaps not the verdict he wanted, but one that allowed her to go free."

"Um!" Sir James frowned thoughtfully. "I wonder why he helped her? I also wonder that he himself escaped suspicion —"

"Oh, he didn't entirely," said Lorna quickly. "But when it came to checking up it was all clear from the doctor's evidence that when the barrister rang the police, Cardine must have been dead for several hours. That meant that he had been killed between one and two a.m., probably earlier, and the barrister had a watertight alibi — he had been playing cards with his friends until nearly four a.m., when he had left with a man from whom he had parted outside the building where he lived. So — though it came out afterwards that he and Cardine were anything but friendly, he was free of all suspicion."

"But, my dear Lorna!" exclaimed Mrs. Marston. "How on earth did you learn all the details of this sordid story — and why should you be so interested?"

"Well — like Cynthia, I'm a thriller fan, and I was intrigued about the non-proven business." Lorna sounded apologetic now. "I couldn't help being tempted to ask Sir James. But Sir James, don't *you* think the Stewart girl got off rather lightly?"

"Maybe. It's an interesting case," replied Sir James. "I'd like to look into it more closely. No doubt it would all have been reported in the newspapers up there."

"It was. As a matter of fact, I looked it up," said Lorna.

"But how on earth did you hear of it in the first place?" demanded Blair, who had listened to the story with a mixture of boredom and annoyance.

"Well —" She seemed to hesitate. "I was at a party the other evening, and someone started talking about unsolved murders, and someone else who knew all about this told us the story. But apart from my curiosity over the verdict, the sequel interested me enormously. You see, it appears this girl changed her name and is actually leading a most exemplary life, and what's more — and what seems to me rather awful, she's going to get married — there's no harm in this because no one knows the names of the people most closely involved. It is of particular interest to me, though, because the man this ex-criminal is going to marry is a doctor. Of course, he doesn't know about her past — "

"Why should he?" asked Blair. "If she's made good, the poor thing deserved to be left in peace — the Cardine man was evidently a complete wrong 'un. Probably deserved to be shot — and though I know no more about the case than anyone here — except apparently yourself — it seems quite possible that she was completely innocent."

"Oh, Blair, dear!" Lorna sounded horrified. "Of course she wasn't! The man was her lover — and as the prosecution tried to prove — they quarrelled over some other woman, and she shot him in a fit of jealous rage. How would you like to find out your wife had that kind of past, and — "

"Just a moment." Sir James was still using his legal mind. "Was there any proof she had ever possessed a revolver, or could use it?"

"No doubt she possessed one, and she had to admit that when she was young she had sometimes gone rabbit shooting with a schoolboy friend. So if she could use a gun, why not a revolver?"

"But, Lorna." Ian Egerton spoke for the first time. "What on earth made the jury doubt her guilt? It's as plain as the proverbial pikestaff."

"Well — " Lorna tried not to sound reluctant, "it seems that one of the windows of the room opened on to the fire escape, and it was wide open. Someone could have entered and left that way though there were no finger-prints of any kind on the window frame."

"There you are," said Blair impatiently. "The whole case collapses. There could easily have been some unknown man, or woman, who committed the crime."

"Then why was the Stewart girl in such a state of dither and — semi-undress. Her dress was torn — "

"Really, Lorna! Must we talk about this for the rest of the afternoon?" asked Mrs. Marston, not attempting to hide her annoyance. "Jean, dear, your tea has gone quite cold. Let me throw it away."

There was still hot water in the silver kettle which was part of the al fresco tea equipage, but Jean refused to have her cup refilled. And after the conversation had changed to different subjects for a short time Lady Drummond rose.

"We really must be getting back," she said. "Don't forget we have dinner guests this evening, James."

"My goodness, so we have. I had forgotten!" Sir James exclaimed, and bidding Lorna goodbye a few moments later: "Well now, young woman, you know about a non-proven verdict!"

She smiled ruefully. "I'm in the doghouse!" she told him in an aside. "Auntie thinks I showed shocking bad taste in talking about it. But don't you agree with me? Isn't it rather awful to think what a scandal could break if people found out about that girl after she got married?"

He patted her shoulder paternally. "You can't do anything about it. . . . All right, dear! I'm coming—" he called in answer to his wife's urgent: "James!"

But rejoining the Egertons, Lorna was far from dissatisfied with the prospect of the damage which the bomb she had planted that afternoon was bound to cause.

Chapter 14

I

Blair and Mrs. Marston went to see the Drummonds off, while Lorna accompanied her friends to their car. Annette, who had shown every sign of boredom, and not said a word during Lorna's recital, looked after her cousin in frowning disapproval. "Why on earth did Lorna want to tell that unsavoury story?" she asked. "Surely she could see Mummy didn't like murder being the sole subject at the tea table." She added abruptly: "Jean, I don't know about you being sunburnt. You look pale to me. Is your head aching?"

"A little. I think I'll go in and tidy up, and perhaps take an aspirin. I have some. Tell Blair I won't be long, will you?" Jean turned towards the house, finding it difficult not to run. She felt that unless she could be alone, it would be impossible any longer to sustain her unnatural self-control.

The hall was empty; crossing it, she ran upstairs, and in a few moments was shut in the Blue Room.

Her wedding-dress still lay over the day-bed, and the sight of it was like a thousand knives in her heart. She would never wear that dress now; how mad and wrong to have dreamed that she could. All the doubts, the vacillations for which she now despised herself, had been solved from the moment when Lorna began her cynically dramatic resumé of Jean Stewart's story.

There was only one clear thing in the chaos of Jean's mind. Moving restlessly about the room, after a little while she stopped beside the window, and standing there staring across to the wood where such a short time ago she had walked with Blair, and felt the wonderful happiness his love brought her, she began to live over again those moments of torture during which she had been forced to listen to Lorna telling that subtly distorted version of what had happened in an Edinburgh court of law nearly seven years ago: the story of a young girl who had passed through an agony of fear and shame that would scar her for the rest of her life.

It came crowding back across the years with such frightening clearness. What a fool she had been to believe Jean Stewart could remain dead and buried, while Jean Campbell lived. That poor little Jean, who had so innocently and loyally believed in the handsome, brilliant man whom she had been so proud to be allowed to help with his work.

How many members of her sex had trusted Ronald Cardine—though perhaps never with his young secretary's devoted belief. He had been nearly twenty years older than she was, and she had never thought of him as a lover for an instant. In these permissive days, when even childhood's innocence is being steadily corrupted by so-called "liberal" thinkers, she knew bitterly that there would be less people to believe the truth about her. What would Blair believe?

Suddenly she knew it was not his belief that she might have killed Cardine that would matter—she did not think for a moment he would believe it. It was that other thing she dreaded him believing, for if she saw the warmth in his eyes fade, knew that his faith in her had died, that would bring her to the ultimate outer darkness.

Young, idealistic fool that I was! she thought.

To have been so proud when her hero had repeatedly told her how helpful she was to him; that he didn't know what he would do without his "perfect little secretary", because she "understood his moods so well!"

To a curiously unawakened seventeen he had seemed almost to fulfil the role of the father she had lost. Sometimes the more than unconventional behaviour of his friends had worried her, but realising it would appear priggish to show her reaction, and persuading herself that these clever people

148

had different standards to those among whom she had been brought up, she had persuaded herself there was no real harm.

It was useless to reproach herself afterwards, and realise what a ninny she had been not to understand that Cardine's casual affection had been the very opposite of paternal. But on the night of his death when she had said goodnight and prepared to go, and he had pulled her roughly into his arms, she had been forced to understand what kind of response he expected.

Her lips bruised, her dress torn, she had rushed across the landing and locked herself in the bedroom, cowering there while he knocked and demanded she should let him in.

Then suddenly he had stopped and she knew he had returned to the other room. Soon after that she had heard voices, and knowing someone was with him, ventured to open the door and listen. She saw that the sitting-room door was shut, and seizing her opportunity, made her silent dash for liberty. Fearful of the sound of the front door shutting, she had left it open; and, her one idea to get away, made her panic rush out of the building not caring what the man whom she had met on the stairs thought, indeed hardly knowing she had encountered him. Her only clear thought was that she must never see Cardine again, and by the time she arrived back at her lodgings she had made up her mind to go straight to old Alison Macrae, who had been her dead mother's friend, and after Mrs. Stewart's death had kept house for the bereaved widower and his motherless daughter.

She thanked heaven that Miss Macrae had moved right away from the island where she, Jean, had been born, to a place where no one knew her. Anyhow, old Alison would have done anything in the world for her.

But before she could even begin to get away, the police had called to interview her, and the ordeal had begun in which the advocate who had been Cardine's neighbour — Neil McNairn — was to prove her only friend; for Miss Macrae had been taken seriously ill and could not go to her.

If she had been less numbed with sheer terror, she might have felt more surprise at the way McNairn had come to her rescue; she hardly knew him, though she had met him several times at parties to which Cardine had taken her; but he was not on intimate terms with the writer and she had sometimes thought the two men rather disliked each other.

As Lorna had insisted, the evidence against the prisoner seemed damning, for in spite of Jean's story of hearing someone else with Cardine, there was absolutely no proof that she was speaking the truth.

It was McNairn's brilliant defence which, after some disagreement among the jury, had finally sent Jean Stewart out into the world again—free, but carrying the stain of the refusal to decide definitely whether she was innocent or guilty of murder.

The story had made glaring headlines in the Scottish newspapers, so it did not surprise Jean that Lorna, having admitted she had "looked it up", knew so much of it. At first she had wondered if it could have been Neil McNairn who betrayed her, but when she remembered what he was like in these days, the unlikelihood of him coming into contact with anyone like Blair's cousin seemed—apart from any other factor—to eliminate him. And had not Jean reminded herself that other people who had known her in Edinburgh might recognise her, changed though she was?

As for that postscript about her career and forthcoming marriage, Lorna did not need to invent that, Jean decided; she knew it and had simply added it to the story.

A tap on the door brought Jean from her unhappy reverie, drawing a sharp little cry from her. Then while the permission to enter stuck in her throat, the door opened and Lorna walked in.

II

The brief seconds in which the two girls faced each other seemed to Jean to last for ever.

Then Lorna broke the silence.

"Well?" The upward inflection made a question of the monosyllable.

Jean answered that question with another. "Why did you choose that way of telling my story?" she asked.

Lorna had expected a broken figure; tears; pleading. If she was disappointed, she was still certain she had the upper hand.

"I thought," she said with cold contempt, "that it was the kindest way to show you the red light. After all, I could have gone to Blair, but I wanted to make sure that he saw the reaction of other people. And that you had time to realise how impossible it was for you to marry him. Surely you know a scandal like that about his wife is hardly the kind of thing a man in his position could afford to have put in circulation? It is up to you to finally decide whether I shall let him know that you are the heroine of my 'thriller'." Then her coolness suddenly turning to scorching venom: "How dared you trap him like that, you—you damned adventuress! I knew from the beginning what your game was; that you were out to get him. I warn you that I'll stop at nothing to prevent any risk of his marrying you—"

"That is a risk that will never be taken," Jean answered. "I am not likely to let him marry me now."

"So you say. But even if you are scheming for—some way of getting round it, I shouldn't try, if I were you."

"Please let us end this discussion," said Jean quietly. "Would you mind going?"

"I certainly have no desire to argue with you." Lorna's eyes narrowed. "Only, I warn you for the last time—get out of Blair's life. He's a dear, chivalrous fool, as no doubt you know; but rather than let him marry you—"

"Can't you see that you have made that quite impossible?" Jean asked.

But had she? Lorna was silent. A new and disturbing thought occurred to her. "Listen," she urged. "Do you really care anything about him, or have you been just using him as security for yourself?"

Jean looked at her, a flicker of contempt in her eyes. "Do you really dare to ask me that?"

151

"Very well; prove it in the only way you can," said Lorna. "Don't give him a chance to ruin himself by insisting on sticking to you. Oh, of course," she added vindictively, "I don't doubt that he is human enough to hate the idea of you and that other man, and it might change him. I don't suppose, in fact, that he would really ever feel quite the same to you." For the first time she knew that she had got under her rival's skin, and seeing Jean's teeth close hard on her underlip, rejoiced in her mean little heart. She knew that she herself was taking a risk, and that she must somehow stop Blair from knowing that she was the cause of his losing the girl who, in her own words, he was besotted with.

"If you really love him, you won't tell him you are Jean Stewart," she said.

"What! Are you crazy?" Jean demanded. "Why have you done what you have if you don't want him to know—"

"Listen," commanded Lorna. "I took the—the kindest—" no wonder the words stuck in her throat, "way I could to make you understand how wicked you were. Can't you see that there is only one way to make things easy for Blair? You must go right away—just disappear out of his life. Write, if you like, and tell him you find you don't care for him, or—anything to save him. If you don't, I'll do as I threaten—"

"And make the scandal you want to avoid for him?" asked Jean. Suddenly this all seemed quite unreal; it was as though she was listening to the plans for someone else's life to be broken to bits.

Everything cruel in Lorna was enjoying this, but she knew she had to tread carefully, and she managed to conjure up something like a note of sympathy as she said: "I don't want you to force me to do that. I do see that you had some excuse, but if you really love Blair you will do as I suggest. The blow to his pride will help him to get over loving you." Her voice hardened again. "It's the only way. You must go."

It did not occur to her that her reasoning, and her mixture of threat and cajolery, were muddled. There was, as Jean had discovered in the past, a streak of stupidity in

Nurse Temple. It showed again in her next words: "It will break his heart to learn the truth about you —"

Before any more could be said Blair's voice reached them, calling urgently. "Jean! Jean — where are you?"

As Jean moved instinctively towards the door her companion caught her arm. "I'll give you till tomorrow to decide —" And when Blair called again, Lorna opened the door calling back: "She's here, and coming!"

"Darling!" Blair exclaimed. "I'm afraid I must go back to town at once. A patient I sent into a nursing home yesterday has had a relapse. I'm shattered to rush you off like this, but can you be ready in five minutes?"

She nodded, knowing she could not trust her voice, for the sight of him brought her nearer to breaking down than anything else had done. Without another glance in Lorna's direction she went quickly out of the room.

Lorna was about to follow when looking back she saw the dress and its lovely accessories lying on the day-bed. She stood staring at it, a cruel smile making her mouth ugly.

"That won't be needed now!" she thought. *"Just — too bad!"*

III

During the drive back, if Blair had not been so concerned about his patient and getting back to London as quickly as possible, he would have noticed how silent and pale Jean was while she sat beside him, her hands clenched in her lap.

Was this really their last drive together? The last time she would be with him! Beyond those miles which the car was eating up so much too quickly, all the rest of her life stretched, empty and barren.

As they reached the outskirts of London and the traffic forced Blair to drive more slowly, he glanced round at her.

"We've done that very well," he said, "without too often breaking the speed limit. Tired, darling?"

"Yes — a little," she admitted.

He said uncertainly: "I don't know how long I may be

kept. Would you like to go to my rooms and wait for me, or—"

She knew that she dared not be alone with him. If she broke down, he would get the whole thing from her to-night, and—she had to think.

"Do you mind if I go right home?" she asked. "My head aches rather, and I think I'll go to bed early."

"My dearest. You've had a heavy week and should have been resting," he said contritely. "What a selfish devil I am."

"Indeed you are not," she denied.

"I hate not being able to take you right home," he said frowningly. "But—"

"Of course you can't. Put me down somewhere, and I'll get a taxi."

And so it happened. Ten minutes later, standing on the pavement she watched traffic swallow his car, and hailing a taxi, was driven home.

At any other time the nurse in her would have accepted that his mind was already on the difficult case he had been called back to, accepted the brief touch of his lips brushing her cheek as she got out of the car, as natural. Now she could only ask herself:

"Was that our goodbye?" . . .

Shut in the flat she shed her coat, and going into the sitting-room, sat down wearily on a chair by the table. She had not turned on the light, and it was only when the lamps in the street below glimmered up through the windows that she began to realise the state of shock from which she was suffering; that ever since tea time she had been like some-one who had suffered a knock-out blow. Now her mind was working again, slowly and painfully.

She remembered Lorna's specious argument, most especially that one sentence which had highlighted Blair's chivalry and—his determination.

And it seemed to her suddenly that Lorna must be right. The only way was to go out of Blair's life; somewhere where he would never be likely to find her.

He must not have the chance of refusing to let her go;

there must be no risk of Lorna carrying out her threat. Jean understood the other girl now as she had never done before; she was dumbfounded to realise the intensity of her hatred, and she knew Lorna would stop at nothing.

But while she sat there thinking, and still too shocked to reason, she knew there was one thing she could not bring herself to do.

She must make the real reason clear to Blair. She could never let him think that she had just heartlessly jilted him. Only—she must not see him again.

With kindly Alison Macrae she would have time to think and plan her future, and she would start at once. There was still time to catch the late night train that would take her to Inverness. Fortunately everything was paid up here, in preparation for her giving up the flat soon.

It was only when looking back afterwards that she realised the sudden sheer panic which urged her decision. The old, dreadful sense of pursuit which she had felt when she knew the whole world was against her—before Jean Stewart had been buried and Jean Campbell had come to life.

Getting up she went across to the small writing table, and turning on the lamp, seized pen and paper and began to write:

"Dearest Heart,

"When you read this, I shall be far away. Don't try to find me, I beg. I have been crazy and unbelievably selfish. When you know that it was my story Lorna told this afternoon, you will understand that there must be no risk of the shadow of my disgrace touching you.

"Try to believe that it all happened to a foolishly inexperienced girl, but I neither killed Ronald Cardine nor ever imagined myself in love with him. Above all, believe he was never my lover.

"I have loved one man in my life and will love him until I die. But my dear, my dear, *don't* try to find me.

"Forgive me, and believe that I am ever

"Your Jean."

Her second note was a brief one to Matron, telling her that "circumstances beyond my control make it imperative for me to go away at once", and asking forgiveness for her hasty and premature departure.

The certainty that Matron would be angry over what must appear unforgivable behaviour was just another wound; and she dared not think about Blair's mother and sister.

It only remained for her to pack her essential personal belongings. If she sent Sally Blaker the key she knew she could trust her to take care of the rest, and Sally was devoted to her. Of course she would be puzzled and upset, but she could be depended on not to tell a soul she had heard from her. So that made a third note necessary.

Going to the Highlands would cover her tracks. To this day Blair did not know the whereabouts of the friend she had only mentioned to him. Jean supposed guiltily that she had been frightened to tell him about Miss Macrae, because the old lady was the only person who knew her true identity—except Neil McNairn.

Chapter 15

I

By the time Jean had packed, it was late. Her nurse's training had taken possession again, helping her to do everything that had to be done, in a calmly methodical way. But inside she was in a state of sick panic; that kind of panic which forces its victims to run. Anywhere—anywhere, to escape and hide.

She had just locked the suitcase she was taking with her, when the telephone bell suddenly broke the silence of the flat. For a minute she stood staring at the instrument in horror. Who would ring at this time? Blair? But he must have been back at his rooms long ago, and he had ordered her to go to bed early; it seemed unlikely he would disturb her, yet—

The insistent summons went on, rasping against her frayed nerves, until with a desperate effort she forced herself to answer.

The voice that came across was the operator's.

"Are you Thameside 9950?"

"Yes."

"I have a call from France for you. Will you take it?"

"Yes. Are—" She was about to ask if they were sure they had the right number when she was told: "Go ahead, please."

A sudden thrill of disquiet came to her when she remembered there was only one source in France from which she would expect a telephone call to eventuate, and the vague feeling that this meant trouble had hardly had time to register before the caller's familiar tones reached her.

"Is Sister Campbell there?"

"Speaking—"

"This is John Barrington. Thank heaven I have contacted you at last. I've been trying for ages. Tim is very ill, Sister—"

"Oh, *no*!"

"So ill that I am taking a desperate gamble that you can drop everything and come to him at once."

Shocked and dismayed she began: "But Mr. Barrington, I—"

"Listen, please. I know you are shortly to be married, and I've been trying to get Marston, but he was not at the hospital, or in Harley Street. There's no time to spare. This can be a matter of life and death, and my little chap's calling for you." The deep tones suddenly shook. "Thank God my personal secretary is in London—at the Savoy. I've told him he's to be ready to bring you back with him tonight. Don't fail me, for God's sake!" And as she hesitated. "Hello! Hello!"

"I'm here. Yes, I'll come. But please promise me not to speak to Blair until I have seen you."

"O.K. It isn't Marston I want this time. I've a doctor here. Anderson will wait until he hears from me, or you arrive. Ring him, please. You won't fail me?"

"No."

"Thank you—I must go back to Tim now."

He rang off, leaving her looking blankly down at the telephone. But only for a second; then she dialled the Savoy number. In spite of the shock of the news she had received, her mind was now crystal clear; she was needed to cope with the illness of the child to whom she was devoted. Tim needed her—was calling for her, and her whole business was to get to him; but while she hastily unpacked again to search for her passport, behind this present urgency lay the knowledge that this could be her most sure way of escape. When it came to the point John Barrington would surely give her any help she needed.

It was not until she and Robert Anderson, Mr. Barrington's super-efficient private secretary, were airborne on the special plane which had been standing by, that Jean learned what had been happening. All she had gathered up to then was that Tim was seriously ill with pneumonia.

"Please tell me how this happened," she said. "He should not have been allowed to run any risk—"

It appeared that after Mr. Barrington joined his son at the villa outside Monte Carlo, he had decided to remain there for at least six months. A governess had been engaged to look after the little boy and give him lessons until he was strong enough to go to school. The governess, an Englishwoman, was highly recommended, and had been a great success in her previous post.

"She really was a capable young woman," Anderson said. "But Tim did not take to her from the first; he and I are good friends and he talked to me a lot, mostly about you and Mr. Marston. Like all youngsters—and he's been a bit spoilt since his operation—he could be difficult at times. I gather he was not above comparing you and Miss Sinclair—in a way that did not flatter her! There is no doubt that he was missing you badly, and not feeling very happy or secure. Last week-end his father had to go to Paris, and young Tim chose to be particularly obstreperous. Anyway," the secretary continued, "on the day his father was due back Tim refused point blank to do any lessons. To punish him Miss Sinclair refused to allow him to go to the airport to meet his father. There was a scene, which ended in the governess locking her charge in his bedroom."

It all sounded so unlike that particular child that Jean was sure the girl in whose charge he was must have gone wrong somewhere. She herself could not help a feeling of guilt, for though she had written to him that she and Blair were going to be married, during these last hectic weeks she had almost forgotten him.

But it seemed Miss Sinclair had been used to quite different types of children, and believed in "strict discipline".

"Which," Anderson continued, "I'm all for if it's exercised in the right way. She should have realised that it's healthy when a boy shows signs of the devil in him. Tim did exactly what I would have done at his age, if I'd felt a punishment was overdone. His room is on the first floor, and he got out of the window, clambered down the creeper, and then set off for the airport. But of course he's only just over seven, and not being used to taking himself around, lost himself; and not knowing enough French to ask his way home, found himself stranded —"

As he went on with his story, Jean thought about the horrible things that could happen to children, and it made her cold with horror.

"You see," the secretary explained, "the weather suddenly changed, as it can do in that part of the world. Sunshine gave place to pouring rain and a mistral. Tim, who was wearing a thin silk shirt and shorts, got soaked to the skin."

Meanwhile, convinced that his small son's absence at the airport was due to the weather, John Barrington had arrived home to find the villa in an uproar and Tim missing. Miss Sinclair had entirely lost her head, and instead of contacting the police had gone off in search of him herself. Barrington immediately rang the Prefecture, and heard to his relief that his son had already been picked up by a gendarme to whom he had, wiser than his governess, finally appealed. The next day the boy was running a high temperature, and coughing his heart out. The doctor diagnosed pneumonia; Tim was now very seriously ill and, as Barrington had told Jean, calling for her in his restless delirium.

III

When the car stopped in front of the pink walled house covered with cascading bougainvillaea, John Barrington was waiting on the threshold. He hurried out to greet Jean, taking her hand.

"How is he?" she asked quickly.

"The doctor has just gone," John told her. "He will be back later. The crisis is past, thank God! But the little fellow is terribly weak. He is sleeping, and if he can find you beside him when he wakes—"

Which was exactly what Tim did find. Jean learnt there had been some difficulty over nurses. Yesterday the one on night duty had suddenly become ill, so that her colleague had been almost continuously on duty all day, and then forced to bear the whole brunt of the crisis hours, coping with the night duty. One look took in the girl's white face and her gallant control of dropping eyelids, and Jean ordered her off to bed.

Sitting beside Tim, alert for the faintest movement, her own problems became for the time being of little importance.

For several hours Tim slept soundly; and then became restless, murmuring in his sleep before his eyes opened. When she bent over him, lifting him gently to hold a cooling drink to his lips, he turned petulantly away.

"I want Jean—where's Jean—?"

"Jean's here, darling. Here with you."

With a little gasp he stared up, suddenly wide-eyed.

"Oh!" he whispered. "Is it really—*are* you—"

"I'm here, sweetheart."

His fingers closed on hers. "You won't go away?"

"Of course not," she promised. "I've come to stay with you. Drink this, old man. You've got to get well quickly."

"You bet!" said Tim, with a ghost of the grin she had grown to love.

He was asleep again in a few minutes, and while she watched him she felt a growing gratitude that John Barrington's telephone message had not come just a few minutes later. For she was necessary here; there was work to do that could—keep her sane.

IV

When the doctor came next morning he was delighted to find a very weak but miraculously bright little patient, who was already demanding to know how soon he would be quite well again.

At first Tim did not want Jean to leave his side for a moment, but when it was explained she had come "all the way from London", and had been awake all night, he had let her go, quite happy at her promise that she would come back to him, but not before he remembered to ask the question she was dreading.

"Is my Mr. Surgeon coming to make me *quite* better?"

"Darling, I'm going to make you quite better," Jean said. "You don't need Mr. Marston this time. He's busy looking after all those little boys and girls in Cinderella. Remember?"

"Yes. Did he send me his love?"

She hesitated, but Tim was tiring, and his eyes closed before she could answer.

Looking down at him for a few moments, although the pain in her heart seemed almost unbearable, she found a strange comfort in the knowledge that the child who owed so much to Blair's skill was even now a kind of link between herself and the man she loved, and had irrevocably lost. She knew she had been so right to come here; it was her bounden duty to help Tim regain and maintain the health Blair's skill had given him. If she could do that, she felt it would be completing a trust. Even though Blair knew nothing about it.

She did not see John Barrington until the evening. He, too, was worn out with watching and anxiety, and ordered by the doctor to catch up on some of his lost sleep.

But when he had had a few hours' rest it was characteristic of him to think also of catching up with neglected business, and he was closeted with his secretary until it was time for him to change for dinner.

He sent Jean a message, asking her to dine with him; adding that dinner would not be until half past eight, when he expected that she would be free.

After seeing Tim settled, and leaving the nurse who was taking over night duty to watch over him, Jean went to her room. She would have given a good deal to be able to avoid what lay ahead. She knew, though, that she must talk to John Barrington, and make him understand how necessary it was that Blair should not know of her presence here.

Her bedroom was next to Tim's. Never in her life had she been in such luxurious surroundings, and because she naturally loved pretty things she looked appreciatively round the charming room with its eggshell blue walls, and carpet of deeper tone. Brocaded blue and silver curtains hung at the windows that looked down on to the villa gardens. The whole house was a picture of what riches can do, and for a moment she wondered if Barrington's wife had been responsible for the very feminine décor of the apartment. Then she remembered that he was renting the villa, and when he was in London he had lived, at the Savoy. Had he no permanent roots? If that was so, it was all wrong, she thought unhappily; Tim should have the background of a real home to grow up against.

But she could not help feeling intensely sorry for John Barrington. She had liked him from the first, feeling he was the kind of man money could not spoil; unlike so many of his very rich and successful contemporaries, he was neither power mad, nor spoilt by success.

Discarding the plain grey dress which she had worn all day, she looked at it as it lay on the satin bedspread, her heart contracting with pain. While she was on duty in the sickroom she had worn a white coif over her hair; she wondered now if those clothes were the nearest thing to uniform she would ever wear again.

Changing into one of the frocks she had so hastily transferred to her suitcase last night—in her hurry she had hardly realised what she was taking—as she slipped the soft, gold coloured material over her head, she realised that the dress was one belonging to the trousseau which she had collected with such loving care. Suddenly memory swept her relentlessly back to that room at Arleigh Hall, and she was remembering the shimmering ivory and silver of that other dress, and again the folly of her hopes and dreams taunted her . . .

163

With a final glance at her reflection, which her training to make sure she was perfectly neat made second nature, she went out of the room.

She had reached the hall before she realised that she had no idea of the lay of the villa, or which room she was expected to enter. While she hesitated a servant came through one of the doors, and seeing her, requested:

"This way, if you please, mademoiselle," and ushered her into her host's presence.

John Barrington was standing by a low table on which the ingredients for before-dinner aperitifs were arranged. Hastily putting down the bottle he was holding, he moved to greet her.

"Here you are. Come and sit down, and tell me what has been happening. I have been trying to catch up on things all day, and until twenty minutes ago I was tied up with a long and complicated telephone call. When I looked in on Tim just now, the nurse told me he had just settled down and she didn't want him disturbed. I hope he won't think I'd forgotten him."

"He isn't thinking very clearly about anything yet," said Jean. "But he has had a wonderfully good day. I'm sure he will be quite ready to talk to you in the morning."

"Don't suppose he will worry about me so long as you are with him." There was a wistful note in his tone that made her suddenly sorry for him when she realised that since her arrival, Tim had not even asked for him. She had commented to Blair, in the boy's hospital days, that though Barrington adored his son, and Tim was undoubtedly very fond of his father, he had often seemed curiously detached, and Blair had said:

"I suppose the poor little chap has got so used to Barrington going off here and there, while he is left with his nurse or his aunt, that he has developed a built-in independence. Even when the mother was around, he must have been very much on his own. But he takes it quite philosophically that he should be. You can't expect a really close relationship in that kind of situation."

"No wonder the doctor says you are a near miracle

worker," Barrington told her now. "Good heavens! I never dreamt Tim could be so far on the road to recovery, so soon."

"I am not really responsible for that," Jean reminded him. "After all, the worst was over before I arrived."

He shook his head. "There was still the chance of a relapse. It's having his beloved 'Jean' that has strengthened his resistance. What will you drink? Sherry? A dry martini — ?"

"Sherry, please."

Turning back to fill a glass for her, he said: "I am annoyed with myself. I meant to let you know that if you wanted to ring London, the telephone was completely at your service. Since I came here, I've had extra lines installed."

"Thank you," she replied, knowing that another dreaded moment was at hand. "I shall not want — need, to ring London."

He looked round. "What about getting in touch with that young man of yours? I'm sure he would rather hear your voice than wait for the post!"

Taking the glass from him, she avoided his eyes. "No. I shall not be in touch with Blair."

Barrington paused in the act of mixing his own drink. Looking across, he saw how pale she had gone, and that the hand raising the wine to her lips was unsteady enough for some of the sherry to spill.

Puzzled, he asked: "Is Marston away then? I couldn't get hold of him when I rang, but I understood he was simply out. Then I got the hospital and they gave me — after some hesitation — your number. I was relieved to find you were still there, because knowing you were going to be married I was scared you might have gone right away somewhere."

There was no help for it, and it was better to get it over quickly. "I have left the hospital, Mr. Barrington. Do you remember that I asked you particularly not to be in touch with Blair until I saw you?" she said.

"Yes." He laughed uncertainly. "Matter of fact, that

was why I didn't let Marston know you had arrived safely—"

She met his eyes steadily. "Mr. Barrington, I am not going to marry Blair. And I am not going back to St. Catherine's—ever."

"What!" He stared at her. "But I thought—Look here! What's wrong?"

There was a moment's silence before she could bring herself to answer:

"I am trusting you to help me. I—hope you will."

"My dear girl, there is nothing possible in this world that I would not do for you," he told her, and there was no mistaking his sincerity. "But what is wrong? Have you and Blair quarrelled?"

She shook her head. "No. Only—I am not going to marry him."

"But—"

"I am relying on you," she interrupted urgently. "And if you feel under any obligation to Blair, you will do as I ask. Because I ask it for his sake. I can't explain. Only, please do as I beg you. Don't let him know that you have been in touch with me, either now or in the future—"

"But what has happened?" John Barrington insisted. He had brought his glass across. He sat down in the chair next to her. "You've broken your engagement? Oh, but it will come right."

She shook her head. "No. If you like Blair, if you think you owe him any debt, *please* do as I ask."

"Of course—if you ask it. Listen to me though. Marston is deeply in love with you. I knew that before you did—perhaps before he knew it himself. It stuck out a mile; I was not in the least surprised when you wrote and told Tim that—you were going to marry his 'Mr. Surgeon'. So—"

She interrupted: "I can only pray Blair will forget me, and find someone more worthy of him. Oh!" She put down her empty glass, twisting her hands together. "Please believe that to marry me would be the worst thing that could happen to him. I beg you not to ask me more now. I trust you. And I need your help."

"It's yours to the last ditch. Are you sure, though, that you are not spoiling his whole life?"

"Not as I should do—" She made a hopeless gesture. "This must all sound very mysterious, but I cannot bring myself to tell you more—at present. I will stay with Tim until he is well; then I want to go right away somewhere." She leant towards him, laying a hand on his arm. "Please believe me when I tell you that if I married Blair, it might bring not only unhappiness, but disaster."

"Of course I will do as you ask," said John Barrington. "If you will stay with Tim now, I will help you to do whatever you want to—afterwards. Here's my hand on it."

She put her hand into the one he extended, and for the first time felt a little comforted.

Chapter 16

I

At the sound of an imperative knock on her office door, Miss Caroline Hilton—"Matron" to everyone at St. Catherine's, looked towards it, a slight frown deepening at the interruption, as the door opened before she had time to give her permission to enter.

Then recognising the early morning disturber of her routine, her expression changed.

"Good morning, Mr. Marston," she said, sounding a good deal more calm than she felt. "I was on the point of trying to find out if you had arrived yet. I am anxious to—"

But Blair's good manners had gone to the four winds, and he interrupted harshly: "Where is Jean? What has happened to her?"

"I was hoping," said Matron, "that you would be able to tell me."

"Then you know that she has gone. Where is she? For heaven's sake tell me."

"I wish I could," she replied. "I hoped you might be able to tell me."

Seeing the strained pallor of his face, the dismay which she had felt before he arrived crystallised into anger. They were old friends and, apart from her affection for him, she thought a great deal of his splendid work here in the hospital, and wherever else he was needed.

"This came this morning." She pushed the piece of notepaper across her desk.

Picking up the note he read it through at a glance; his face was almost expressionless, but when he raised his eyes she saw the misery in them.

"Is that all?" he asked. "She wrote to me too." Though he knew he could trust her implicitly, he had no intention of discussing the reasons Jean had given him.

"Do you mean to tell me," Matron questioned, "that she gave you no idea she intended to behave like this?"

"Until I got her letter I had no inkling there was anything wrong —"

"She must have gone crazy!" Matron exclaimed angrily.

"No." Blair began to pace the floor. "She has given me a stronger reason for her departure than she gave you. But you must forgive me if I feel I can't discuss that now." He stopped in his pacing, facing her again. "Surely you can help? You must know more about her background than — through my own folly — I have ever learnt. You know where she came from; there must be some address where I can at least get news of her?"

There was a puzzled crease between Matron's brows. "So far as I know she had no relatives. She was a curiously reserved girl. She came here with a strong recommendation from the Matron of the Northern hospital where she had trained, who was an old friend of mine. But Janet Carson has married since, and gone abroad, I don't know where."

"Jean had a relative — or friend, somewhere in the Highlands, I think."

"I know nothing about that."

He sighed. "I hoped you might be able to help."

"I wish I could," she said. "The whole affair is inexplicable. Jean is the last person I would have dreamed of ever turning hysterical."

"She has got it into her head that she ought not to marry me." His voice hardened. "Something that happened yesterday put it there. However, I must not take up your time. There is only one thing," he added, turning when he reached the door. "If you possibly can, I should like you to make some excuse for her sudden departure to the rest of the staff. I should be terribly grateful if you could make things sound as normal as possible."

She hesitated. As Matron, she felt that personal affairs, whatever they might be, should be subordinate to a nurse's duty and the hospital's needs. For a senior, with an important job of work to do, to walk out on her job like this, appeared quite inexcusable. But she realised that Blair would hate a lot of talk and comment, and after all, apart from her liking for him, he was a senior consultant.

"Fortunately," she said, "I had made all arrangements to replace Sister Campbell. She would have left on Saturday, so I *can* say that an emergency arose that made it necessary for me to release her at once."

"Thank you." Blair went out, shutting the door. His mouth was set grimly while he made his way along the corridor to his office, still cursing himself for not having guessed last night that something was very wrong. Yet how could he have known that the story Lorna had told in his mother's garden, was connected in any way with Jean. Such a thing had never occurred to him. And now he was torn apart between fury at what he rightly considered his cousin's treachery, and his love and pity for the beloved girl whose loss would leave a blank in his life which nothing in the world could ever fill.

He must find Jean; she must come back to him. Blair had learnt to read men and women very accurately, and he told himself that he was not likely to be wrong where the person he loved best was concerned. Not for any moment did he doubt her innocence. But it was not without bitterness that he asked himself why she had not given him a chance to make his own decision; to convince her that no threat of scandal, or even the risk of losing his whole career, would ever have induced him to give her up. Somehow she must be convinced of that. What he was in no state to understand was that it was because she knew it that she had gone away.

His eyes cold as steel, he reached for the house telephone. Whatever breach of hospital etiquette he was committing, he was determined to talk to Lorna without loss of time.

"Mr. Marston speaking. Send Nurse Temple down to my room at once, please," he told the young nurse who answered, and without waiting for a reply, replaced the telephone and sat fuming until the expected knock on his door came, and in answer to his peremptory "Come in", Lorna entered.

She had been told: *Mr. Marston was on the telephone. He wants to see you at once. He sounds livid.* But being a fundamentally stupid person, it was only with a slightly excited expectation that she had hurried to obey the summons.

"You wanted me, Blair?" she asked.

"I *sent* for you," he corrected.

"Yes?" Meeting the ice in his look, a thrill of dismay made her heart beat more rapidly.

"How *dared* you tell that story yesterday?" he demanded. "What right had you to spy so despicably on Jean?"

So she had told him! Somehow Lorna had never believed that would happen. She had thought Jean would do anything rather than have him know the truth. Her eyes shifting, she stammered: "I—I don't quite understand—"

"Oh, yes you do!" His voice, usually so charming, was like a whiplash. "You knew whose story it was. What the hell right have you to pry into Jean's life?"

This angry man was like a stranger—frightening in his suppressed violence. But spite swamped her dismay, helping her to recover from the shock.

"So she did tell you that she was the heroine of my little history," she said softly. "Rather late to confess, wasn't it? But of course she was afraid that if she did not tell you, I would."

"And why should you?" he asked, so harshly she flinched back from him. "What possible business was it of yours? How could you be sure that I was not in possession of the facts already?"

"Dear Blair, you were not. Oh," her tone became pleading, "why should you be angry with me for trying to save you? It would have been criminal to stand by and let you walk into the trap that designing bitch had laid so cleverly."

"Please keep to facts, and do not allow your very cheap sense of drama to run away with you," he said bitingly. "Answer my question. What right had you to interfere between the girl I am going to marry and myself?"

"But Blair, you can't marry her!" Lorna exclaimed.

"Can't you see it was because I knew such a step would ruin you that I took that way of warning her off? Can't you see that it is my business—the business of anyone who cares for you? You had to know. Of course she had very cleverly played on your feelings for her, but you are not a fool."

"No," he agreed. "I am not. And so I am unlikely to believe for one moment that Jean is guilty of the accusation which—"

"You must be mad!" she interrupted. "Why, she has never been really cleared of suspicion—"

"Be silent!" he ordered.

But she was in a panic now. Had Jean really got round him? Did he still mean to marry her? "I won't!" she said defiantly. "Of course you're crazy about her. No doubt that dead man was too. No, Blair! Let me speak! Can't you understand how impossible it is for you to bring a creature like that into the family? Think. If the story ever comes out—"

"As you would take every care it should!"

"Yes, I would!" she flung back at him, sure now that her only remaining chance of success would be if she did not weaken. "I might have known she would have come whining and lying to you!"

"Will you be silent!"

"No! Blair, if you won't listen to any kind of reason, think of the shock it would be to your mother if it ever became known that your wife had been—not only tried for murder, but was the mistress of the man whom she killed!"

"That is a lie!" He did not raise his voice, but though she was not so insensitive that she did not sense danger in his very quietness, sheer jealous hatred of Jean drove her on.

"Ask anyone to believe that. Working late! Innocent girls don't stay in a man's rooms doing secretarial work into the small hours! Don't make me laugh! When you come to your senses, you will admit that I took a very generous way of showing her the red light."

Blair regarded her in silence for a moment. If she had been a man he would have known exactly how to deal with her, and even now it was difficult to keep his hands off

172

her; he could be dangerous, like so many men of a normally quiet disposition, once his temper was unleashed. Though the fact that he had practically seen her grow up had made him regard Lorna with a not always tolerant kind of family affection, he realised now that he had endured rather than liked her. If anyone had hinted to him the plan she had formed regarding their future relationship, he would have been amazed, and he was therefore quite unable to find any reason for her now open antagonism to Jean.

"It would interest me to know from whom you unearthed this preposterous story," he said. "It must have taken quite a lot of detective work."

"I didn't need to spy on her." If she was beginning to realise that what she had done could act like a boomerang, Lorna was still determined to stand firmly by her action. Somehow Blair had got to be convinced how mad it would be to let Jean remain in his life. "It was a lucky chance — Fate, I believe — that put the whole thing in my way. But I'm not going to pretend that I ever liked or trusted her. She can take other people in, but remember I've worked with her."

"Spare yourself the trouble of going into that kind of detail, and answer me," Blair ordered.

"Very well," she agreed sulkily. "I called at her flat on Friday evening. (I never liked her, but I was determined to try to — be nice to her, because of you.) She was out when I arrived, and there was another caller waiting on the mat. A drunken, disreputable ex-barrister who fastened himself on me, wanting me to buy him a drink. You should thank me for my curiosity about him; if I had not got better acquainted with Mr. Neil McNairn, my omission could have proved disastrous."

"Well?" He showed no sign of the shock he felt. So that was how it had happened!

She continued: "The man is a confirmed alcoholic, but when he's stoned, he doesn't pass out, or anything like that. He just talks. He became boringly reminiscent about the story of his life — at least it was boring at the beginning. He almost wept over his ruined career; then he went on to describe his greatest triumphs. Had I ever heard of the Cardine murder case? Ah, that was a triumph for him! He recited the whole story of it. Frankly, I found myself rather enthralled! I asked what became of the girl, and did he think she was really guilty? He said if it hadn't been for the great defence he put up for her, she would certainly have been adjudged so. Anyhow, she was grateful to him. And he met her again just recently. 'Here in London?' I asked. He became mysterious then, but another whisky made him confidential. He said the sequel wouldn't be believed if it was written in a book. Would I believe 'the lassie' had made good. Become a nurse in a children's hospital and was going to marry a great doctor, bless her! 'Yes, yes, Jeannie Stewart had made good'. I'm not a fool, Blair," Lorna continued. "And—suddenly it all seemed to fit in. After all, Jean was a nurse in a children's hospital, and he had been calling on her that evening. I asked him outright if the name of his ex-client was not Jean Campbell. I must say he sobered then and shut up like a clam. I left him looking pretty shattered."

Sick with disgust, remembering the man he had met at Jean's flat, and realising how, plying him with drink, Lorna must have determinedly encouraged McNairn to talk, it seemed to Blair as though he could see and hear the man's maudlin egotism becoming more and more inflated as he recited the story of his "triumph", while his companion took care to get him to a state when he could keep nothing to himself.

"You see," Lorna urged eagerly, mistaking the reason for her companion's silence: "That man knows, and if he would talk to me, he'd talk to other people. He's even capable of blackmailing you. I am sure that he has had money from Jean. I suppose she has been paying him to keep quiet." Going round the desk she laid a hand on Blair's shoulder, continuing pleadingly: "Blair—my dear. I know you hate me now, but one day perhaps you will realise how deeply I care for your happiness. I would do anything to save you from such a marriage, and all the risks it would have brought—"

174

Raising one of his own hands he removed hers. There was nothing violent about the action, but there was something frighteningly definite.

"Blair!" she pleaded, panic stirring in her again. "Don't hate me—"

He said: "I don't 'hate' you. I simply hope I need never see you again. For the rest—you can tell the story all over London if you want to. It will make no difference to me. You have succeeded, in your petty spite, in driving Jean away from me for the moment; but if I have to follow her to the edge of the world, I shall find her, and marry her." He paused, then added with biting emphasis: "Just now you spoke of my mother. When she knows what you have tried to do, you will find that never again will you be allowed to cross the threshold of Arleigh. She, no more than myself, will be ready to condemn Jean, and she will be quite unable to forgive your stupid and malicious mischief making. So far as we—my mother, myself, and most certainly Annette—are concerned, you will cease to exist. Now get out!"

She looked at him, her face whitening. Never, in all her scheming, had she dreamed of this consequence of her spite. She knew that her aunt regarded her with only tepid affection, while with Annette she had never been on anything but the coolest of terms. But she had, as she had stated earlier, her share of family pride; and the knowledge that she would never be welcome at Arleigh Hall again was like a knife twisting in her self-esteem.

"Blair, you can't—" she began. But the words died on her lips as she met the iron hardness of his stare. Without another word she turned and went out of the room.

But when she shut the door, though her hands were shaking, the thought came to her that however little he wished to see her again, Blair would still be forced to do so in the course of work. And if Jean had really gone (what a relief the thought brought!), there might yet be a chance to convince him that she, Lorna, had acted for the best—

And then, remembering the bleak dislike in Blair's eyes,

the cold finality of his voice, a wave of rage and frustration swept over her.

But if she had failed, she told herself savagely, at least those two were parted. And perhaps — he would never again succeed in finding Jean. . . .

II

Jean stood on the terrace of the low, pink walled house overlooking the marvellous blue of the Mediterranean. Though autumn was well on its way, the villa gardens were still a riot of colour, and the sparkling sun-filtered air was filled with the perfume of flowers. Outside the gates the Grande Corniche wound its way to near-by Monte Carlo, that paradise of the jet set — those international playboys and their feminine counterparts.

Jean seldom went into Monte Carlo, but behind the flower draped walls enclosing John Barrington's temporary home, she had found, for a little while, the sanctuary she needed. She was protected by the solemn promise Tim's father had given not to betray her whereabouts. But there was no escape from the memories that haunted and tortured her day and night. Did she want to escape? When those memories were all that were left her of the man for whom her love only grew stronger as the passing weeks drew her further away from him.

Would Blair be able to forgive her? Or would he believe, in spite of her denial, that that other man had been her lover?

Her sense of duty and her affection for Tim had persuaded her to turn her back on her original plan to go to Scotland and find shelter with her old friend until she could manage to start yet another new life, in some country far overseas where no shadow from her past could ever harm the man she loved so dearly.

Meanwhile, she knew that she had found a friend in John Barrington. The more she saw of him, the more she admired the integrity which he had kept throughout what must have been a difficult life. As she got to know him, it seemed more tragic that his riches should have failed to bring him the companionship and happiness every man needs. In spite of all the people who passed through his life, he was a lone wolf; he appeared to have no intimate friends, and only one object in life except his work — Tim. Jean's own loneliness made her terribly sorry for him. She knew that he had a great liking for Blair, but since she had confided in him he had not mentioned the other man's name again.

It had not been so easy with Tim. At first it added to her torture to have the little boy continuously asking about his beloved "Mr. Surgeon". Of course he had wanted to know when she and Blair were going to be married. She had explained that it was "put off" because "Mr. Marston was too busy to get married; much too busy to come to France, even to see his friend Tim."

But lately Tim had stopped talking of Blair, and she hoped that perhaps he was resigned to the thought of not seeing his friend. Jean understood children so well that at any other time she would have discovered how hurt her small charge was at never receiving a letter or a message from Blair, whom he naturally thought must know he had been ill; he was a strange child and had learned, like his father, to keep many things to himself.

While she watched him now, driving his magnificent miniature motor-car round the garden paths, there was a sudden new pain in her heart, for she knew the time was drawing near when she would have to leave him; her way did not lie in this scented oasis; she must go out into the world again, and find real work to fill the emptiness of her life.

John Barrington had been away for the last week, but was expected back that evening. She had no idea where he had gone, but he was always flying off somewhere, and what worried her most was what would be done with Tim when she had gone.

"I'm going in now, darling," she called. "Don't forget tea in half an hour."

"O.K." Tim called back. But when the half hour was

nearly up and she looked out of the window to call him in, there was no sign of her charge. She sent the maid who waited on the schoolroom in search of him; but before Thérèse returned, Tim came running towards the house from the opposite direction and in a few moments arrived in the schoolroom. Excusing his lateness, he informed her: "I went to post a letter to a friend of mine." When he added: "Very important!" she smiled indulgently, knowing how whole-heartedly he flung himself into the games he made up.

"Was it to the Queen?" she asked — the Queen being a favourite make-believe correspondent of his.

Tim shook his head. "I'll tell you later. It's a big secret — you'll be so surprised — and pleased — when you know." Plainly he did not mean to take her into his confidence, and tactfully she left it at that.

John Barrington returned late that evening, and on the next one Jean went downstairs to dine with him.

After dinner, when they were having their coffee, Barrington told her abruptly: "I looked in on London on my way back, and saw Marston."

Startled, she stammered: "Blair! You did not — "

"It's all right," he said. "I did not tell any secrets."

"I didn't think you would," she said quietly.

Examining the end of his cigar, he added casually: "We spent an evening together. I was feeling a bit browned-off that particular evening. It was — the anniversary of my wedding. He helped me a lot. Come to think of it, he's the only person I'd talk to about my private life — except yourself."

"Thank you for including me," she said impulsively.

"Oh, well." His smile lost its bitterness. "You trusted me — I ought to be able to talk to you." He knew her whole story now, because she felt that he should be told before deciding if he wanted her to stay. "Look, Jean," he continued: "I don't want to hurt you further, but — Marston is very unhappy. He naturally did not tell me about — what you told me. But he did tell me you had broken the engagement. That he had no idea where you were, and that there was no other girl in the world for him. I must say, I felt rather a heel, because I knew any news of you would have helped him. What harm would there be in sending him a line—just to tell him you are safe somewhere."

"I can't!" she exclaimed. "I dare not! It would be post-marked. He'd find me. And he must not. You know that he must not."

"I am not so sure of that. He's lonely. He's eating his heart out."

"Don't!"

But he felt he must go on, even though he knew he was hurting her. Blair's unhappy eyes were haunting him. "Are you letting yourself be chased by fear of a ghost that can never materialise?" he asked bluntly. "If Blair still wants to marry you, if he's ready to take any risk there may be, have you any right to deny him his happiness?"

The old, specious argument! The one she had let Mc-Nairn—of all people in the world—persuade her to listen to. Blair's happiness! But she would not allow herself to be tempted again.

She shook her head. "I know I have chosen the right and the only way. I must never see him or be in touch with him again. For his own sake."

"But what are *you* going to do with your life?" he asked.

She said: "I wanted to talk to you about that. I've been thinking. It is getting time for me to move on, Mr. Barrington."

"Where to?" he asked.

She hesitated, then: "Nurses are wanted all over the world. I thought if I could get to Australia, or somewhere like that."

"You really mean that you are determined not to see Marston again?"

"Quite determined."

"Yet you still care for him?"

"Yes. I shan't stop doing that," she said in a low voice.

"I don't want to be cruel, but it all seems such a ruddy waste," he told her. "Here am I, who gave a woman who didn't want it all I had to give. There are times when the memory of the fool I was, for she never cared a damn about me, Jean, gets me down. But for the rest of the time it's over and done with. The silly part is," he went on thoughtfully, "I've got nothing of that sort left to give. But here are you and Blair Marston breaking your hearts—or anyhow, with your happiness in bits. Something ought to be done about it."

"Nothing can be."

After a pause he asked: "Did you have no friend who might have done something to find out who really did kill Ronald Cardine?"

She stared at him, her eyes widening. "No one would ever have thought of such a thing. You see, I was the suspect. Everything pointed to me. I had every chance of taking the weapon with me, and getting rid of it."

"I know," he said. "I looked up the case. I—forgive my interference — have even had some enquiries made. But it's a dead end. It always has seemed to me that that non-proven business is a two-edged sword. It certainly lets the accused out into the world, but—"

"It doesn't say they are innocent. Don't I know that!" She met his eyes directly. "I wonder what you really think?"

"What I am certain Blair does. That whatever provocation you had, you're as innocent as an unborn babe." But that didn't help her—or Blair, he thought angrily. "So you want to go to Australia?" he asked. "Well, it's a grand country. But what about Tim?"

"Tim? Of course I shall miss him, and love him always. But he'll forget me in time. He'll be going to school."

"Not to boarding school for many years—although of course they fly by," he said. "Tim needs some real background, Jean. Somewhere, even when he's growing up, to go back to. If you and Marston had married, I would have asked you to take charge of him. You are too young to run a house for me—even though I am away such a lot; it's a nasty-minded world, and I wouldn't have people whispering scandal."

To have made a home for Tim, and for this lonely man to

come back to! The idea was as attractive as it was un-expected, but she saw the snag. Should she tell him she did not mind what people said about her? After all, it would be in some foreign country.

He continued thoughtfully: "If I bought a place in Bermuda, I'd be able to see a fair amount of Tim. I've got to put him somewhere. I can't drag him all over the place. I've a lot of interests in that part of the world, but — again you're too young and attractive to keep house for any man, unless—" And when she looked at him en-quiringly: "There's one way, Jean. If you married me."

"Married you!" she exclaimed.

"Wait. It might prove unfair to you. You've got to look at the thing whole. I'm not in love with you, Jean, but I'm very fond of you; grateful to you, and I should be honoured if you would bear my name. Anything you have to give belongs to Blair Marston. I accept that. As far as Blair is concerned, though I don't believe he will ever forget, or can replace you, he will gradually get used to the pain of losing you, and thank God! he still has the work that means so much to him. But Tim adores you, and he needs you. Maybe I need you too. Will you think about it? Don't say yes or no now. Give it a week. A week today. Yes?"

For a few seconds she was silent before she answered: "Yes, John. I—will think about it."

Hearing herself, she felt that she had already lighted the flame that would finally burn her boats, leaving no chance of return.

But what chance was there already?

Chapter 17

I

Why had she not said from the beginning that the arrangement John Barrington had suggested was impossible?

And yet—at least she would be of some use, and know that she was where she was needed. For Tim did need her, and so, in some curious way, did that man with his built-in, inner loneliness.

One part of Jean's mind told her that there must still be some place for her in the profession which had once meant everything to her. But would it be easy to find that place? There were, after all, such things as references—proof that as a nurse and nursing sister she had made good; to present that information she would be obliged to advertise who she was. And even if it was from the other side of the world, if Blair found out her whereabouts, there was the risk that he would follow her.

Years hence that might be quite different. When sufficient time had elapsed, a knowledge that was like a knife turning in her heart told her that John Barrington was right.

"He will gradually get used to the pain of losing you, and thank God, he still has the work that means so much to him . . ."

However much it might hurt her, she felt she ought to pray that prophecy would come true.

Yet it seemed so hard that she must go on paying for someone else's sin!

Since that conversation with John Barrington the days had seemed to fly by with frightening speed, each bringing her nearer to the decision which she had promised to make at the end of a week. And tomorrow the week would be up.

Sitting by the window in her bedroom, the book she had

been trying to read lying neglected in her lap, she knew that to wait, as she had been doing, until the last possible minute to make up her mind, was sheer folly. The time had come when she must decide. Surely if she said yes, there was some other kind of happiness to be found in devoting her life to the child who had never known a mother's love and who clung to her so devotedly. *"You're not going away, Jean. You won't leave me this time?"* Tim had pleaded only yesterday evening when she had put him to bed.

There would never be a child of her own now, to claim that other love which her whole womanhood longed to give. Had she not dreamt one day of holding a son of Blair's in her arms.

With a smothered exclamation she sprang to her feet. She was surely being shown the way her duty lay, and it was cowardly to turn from the path. She would write a note to John now, and tell him her answer was yes. And she would see that the note was delivered to him first thing tomorrow morning.

Once that was done, it would be too late to draw back, whatever happened.

She shut her mind to the thought, and going through the communicating door into her sitting-room, she sat down at the writing desk and began to write rapidly:

"Dear John,
    "I have decided —"

She looked round, oddly startled by a soft knock on the door. Her "Yes, Thérèse?" was a little impatient when the maid appeared.

"Pardon, mademoiselle," the girl said. "There is a gentleman downstairs asking for M'sieur Tim, but he is out in the car with his father."

"I know. Who is the gentleman?" asked Jean.

"He says, a friend of monsieur's, and he is here at the M'sieur Tim's invitation —"

Tim made all kinds of friends, and after a moment's hesitation in which she glanced down at the note she had begun, knowing how much more difficult it could be to write it later, Jean rose unwillingly.

"Very well. I will come down."

A few moments later she turned the handle of the door to the mauve salon, where Thérèse had told her the visitor was waiting.

A tall man was standing staring out through the long open windows. He turned as she entered, and they faced each other. Then:

"My darling. You didn't really believe I wouldn't find you?" Blair asked, his hands stretched out to her.

II

Jean's own hands, going instinctively half way to meet those outstretched ones, dropped to her sides, while she drew back, white and shaken.

"Oh, why have you come?" she asked. "How did you know—" It could not be possible that John Barrington had broken his word to her!

"How did I know where you were?" he asked. "Why, Tim wrote and told me!"

"Tim!" Suddenly she remembered the letter he had been so very mysterious about. But that had been nearly a fortnight ago.

Blair said: "He seemed to take it for granted that I was in touch with you."

"What did he say?" She felt stunned, but behind her shock her heart was beating wildly.

Blair took a folded paper from his pocket. "You can see for yourself. The little chap addressed it simply to 'St. Catherine's, London'. It seems to have been going the round of convents and hostels, and heaven knows where, when I should have thought the first place the postal authorities would have chosen was the hospital. And then I was away when it arrived—or I should certainly have been here before. Thank God it finally did reach me."

She hardly heard him. She was reading what Tim had scribbled in his large, childish writing:

"Dear Mr. Sirjon,

"Could you come an see me? I kno you coodn't while I was ill, and Jean says you are to bizzy to get away. I think she must want to sea you too. She dose not seem very hapy sumtimes. Do come. It's luvly here.

"Your luvin
        "Tim."

She looked up speechlessly, and taking Tim's letter back, Blair's hands closed over hers, drawing her towards him.

"For heaven's sake let us have an end to this!" he said roughly. "You must know how futile it is —"

"No!" She tried to free herself. "Can't you understand? Once and for all, I refuse to risk my disgrace touching you —"

"But my dearest heart," he told her gently, "there is no risk now."

"How can you say that? Oh, please go away." In spite of all her effort, a sob strangled the words.

"My love," said Blair. "That's all over —"

"It isn't. It can never be."

Drawing her across to the sofa he went on: "Sit here and listen to me. Or rather: Read that." This time it was a fairly thick wad of notepaper he offered her.

Taking it she looked down blankly, her sight momentarily blurred. Then as it cleared she recognised the handwriting, which though it lacked all the firmness she had once known, was only too familiar. A stifled cry escaped her. Blair's voice sounded strangely muffled when he told her:

"Yes, darling. That is from Neil McNairn. He wrote it before he died, and —"

"Died!"

"Yes. Wait a moment. Let me explain," he urged. "I had been searching for him ever since I found out it was he who put Lorna on the track of your story. But he had been down into the West Country again, and only returned to London on the day he was knocked down by a car and badly injured. He was not so badly hurt that he might not have recovered if he had been in better shape. But he was a dying man before the accident. He knew it, and that was why he wrote this. He begged the doctor at the hospital where he had been taken to send for me; and when I went, he asked me to go to his lodging and collect an envelope that was addressed to me, from among his papers. He said he didn't expect to be forgiven, but as he was 'done for', the time had come when he wanted you to read what he had always meant you to after he was dead. He asked where you were, and when I said I didn't know, and he learned that you had gone away, he begged me to open the enclosure and read it. It's your turn now."

Her hands unsteady, Jean unfolded the sheets she held, and read the confession of the man who had saved her, and then almost ruined her whole life.

McNairn had written:

"When you get this, Jean, I'll be beyond the punishment I deserve — or having it well served out to me! Even after a lifetime of disbelief, what I had drummed into me when I was young gives me the uncomfortable feeling that some of it might be true. Though no hell can be worse than the one I have known. It hasn't helped to know that if I was not a despicable, sodden coward, I'd have told the truth long ago. The fact is, I persuaded myself it didn't matter, because you'd made good and were going to end up supremely happy. Then I had to get stinking drunk and spill your story to that damned girl. I'm never so far gone that I don't remember what has happened the night before. I was horrified at what I'd done, but I was so ill that day, and afterwards — well, I was too craven to undo it. So I'm writing this because I know the doctors are right and I'll be dead quite soon. I could buy a few months, perhaps a year, they said, if I'd stop drinking, but I'm beyond caring for life.

"Well, let's get on.

"Have you ever wondered why I came and offered to defend you that time? Human kindness — pity for you? Not altogether. When you asked me so often why the real culprit could not be found, *I* was the only person who could have told you. It was because Cardine's murderer was only known to the philanthropic advocate! who put up such a marvellous defence for you, and sent you out into the world to carry the burden of 'the benefit of the doubt'.

"Cardine was killed by the woman whom he had married years before. She was the only woman I ever cared for—if she had chosen me, how different all our lives would have been. But she chose him, and may an eternal curse follow him for what he did to her.

"When I found Cardine that night, she was still there, crouching beside him. Too ill and too shocked to escape the way she had entered the room—by the fire escape (remember the iron steps outside his windows?). But although she was terribly changed, I knew her at once . . ."

Jean looked up from her reading. "Ronald Cardine's *wife?*"

Blair nodded, his expression grim. "Yes. Do you want to read the rest, or shall I tell you?"

"He knew who did it—" She looked down at the paper she held, horror and revulsion filling her. "But—I don't understand. If he knew, how *could* he—Oh, yes, please tell me! I can't bear—" She thrust the rest of the confession away from her, and Blair said:

"He loved her. It is no excuse, but he made it so. He has written that if ever a woman had provocation, Liana Cardine had. She was half Spanish, had been on the stage when Cardine met her. Cardine made her life a hell upon earth. And when she left him he refused to set her free to marry the man she went to. Finally, her lover had died— they were living in France in the greatest poverty. She was half crazy that night, or perhaps she would never have gone to see her husband with every intention of killing him. McNairn says here—" Blair gathered up the scattered sheets of paper, "that he was determined to protect her. He helped her to get away, and shut and locked the window. He did away with all traces of finger-prints, before he called the police. He says it came as a shock to him when the man from the flat below described how he met you on the stairs. But even when you were arrested, he couldn't bring himself to tell what he knew. I think you had better hear the rest in his own words."

She listened intently as Blair read:

"I suppose that if you had been adjudged guilty, I should have done something about it, but I determined to get you off. You see, I knew there was no real proof of your guilt, and I had got rid of Liana's revolver, and sent her to a safe place—she was terribly ill. Then when you were allowed to go free, it seemed I'd done all I could. Liana was already dying of an incurable disease. She died six months later. I didn't care what happened to me after that. I just drank myself into a failure, and when you sink as low as I did, there's nothing left but to sink lower. It was a damnable fate that sent me across your path again at a time when I was down and out. If I hadn't got that money from you, I'd have ended up with a knife in my back from some of my murky acquaintances I'd been in with. I won't even ask you to forgive me, but here's the truth for what it's worth; and if you ever need to use my confession, it will enable you to establish your innocence. That's all.

"Neil McNairn."

Taking Jean's hands again, Blair drew her to her feet. "My dear, the worst of it all is, that you have suffered so much for nothing. Please understand that it's over now. McNairn is dead—he can't blab out his drunken revelations again. No one would ever be likely to connect you with what happened—"

"But Lorna—she knows," Jean protested. "She hates me. She would do anything to stop me marrying you. Let's face it! She wanted you herself."

"Did she?" She hardly recognised the ice hardness of his voice and eyes. "How—interesting." Then, an arm about her, his expression softened. "Don't worry, dear heart; I have already talked to Lorna. I understand that she has now decided to give up nursing, and is going abroad. No doubt she will manage very well, but as far as either myself, or my mother and Annette are concerned, she has ceased to exist."

"Blair!" Jean exclaimed, drawing back in dismay. "Your mother! I haven't dared think how she must feel about me. Coming away as I did, must have made it so—difficult to explain. I didn't think—"

"Don't worry about that. My mama is capable of explaining away any difficult situation!" he assured. "You were called to nurse a sick relation, and our wedding had to be postponed, but only 'postponed'!"

"Can't you see how she would feel if she knew—" Jean began.

"My dear, she does know. Everything." He rose, pulling her to her feet again, and into his arms. "No more of this. Your future is settled—unless you no longer care for me?"

She knew then that she was beaten. But even now, with happiness in her grasp, because she was Jean she had to think of someone else. "Tim," she said. "What's going to happen to him? His father said—told me that if you and I had married, he would have asked us to—take care of him."

"Well, you are going to marry me. So there's nothing to worry about," he said firmly. "We'll be starting out with a half-time family—to be going on with! O.K.?"

"My darling," she replied unsteadily. "I can't believe it—" But his lips were against hers, and she knew it was wonderfully true.

It was some time later when he told her: "By the way, I have not delivered my mother's message yet. 'Her dear love; your wedding dress is still waiting for you. You are to come back *and wear it.*' Which is exactly what you're going to do! Understand, my darling—Doctor's orders!"

FORGET THE DREAM

HERMINA BLACK

Karen Rivington's life had never been easy, especially since her undependable actor father had died, leaving her to look after her younger sister, Corinne. And when the film company she and Corinne were working for packed up and stranded them in South America, it seemed like the final straw.

But all of a sudden their luck changed. For their father's millionaire brother at last succeeded in tracing them, and invited them to share his South American home. At first the girls were in seventh heaven as they travelled to his luxurious hacienda. But when Karen met Gwynne, the handsome, mysterious Englishman who lived as a recluse on a neighbouring estate, she soon found that even wealth and security provide no guarantees of happiness in the most important thing of all, love.

CORONET BOOKS

LOVE FOR FRANCESCA

HERMINA BLACK

Francesca left her job as assistant to a Harley Street doctor in order to go to Morocco. It was the lure of that fascinating country which made her give up her safe London life and travel to Fez as private nurse to a wealthy young beauty.

The young nurse expected excitement of a sort in a city as thrillingly different as Fez. But even Francesca's colourful imagination could not have conjured up the intrigue and danger which was to follow a chance meeting on that first enchanted morning. And even Francesca had no idea how important Julian Beresford was to become in her life.

CORONET BOOKS

ALSO AVAILABLE FROM CORONET

HERMINA BLACK

☐ 20751 5	Forget The Dream	60p
☐ 02477 1	Love For Francesca	50p
☐ 17831 0	The House In Harley Street	30p
☐ 16714 9	Yesterday's Love	30p
☐ 18608 9	Poisoned Paradise	30p
☐ 18301 2	Dangerous Masquerade	30p
☐ 18781 6	Shadows Of Roses	30p
☐ 18810 3	A World Of Shadows	35p
☐ 19480 4	Loren Ruston, S.R.N.	30p
☐ 19829 X	Ballerina	40p

JANE BLACKMORE

☐ 17877 9	It Couldn't Happen To Me	30p
☐ 17878 7	Bitter Honey	30p
☐ 18613 5	A Love Forbidden	30p

All these books are available at your local bookshop or newsagent, or can be ordered direct from the publisher. Just tick the titles you want and fill in the form below.
Prices and availability subject to change without notice.

CORONET BOOKS, P.O. Box 11, Falmouth, Cornwall.
Please send cheque or postal order, and allow the following for postage and packing:
U.K. — One book 19p plus 9p per copy for each additional book ordered, up to a maximum of 73p.
B.F.P.O. and EIRE — 19p for the first book plus 9p per copy for the next 6 books, thereafter 3p per book.
OTHER OVERSEAS CUSTOMERS — 20p for the first book and 10p per copy for each additional book.

Name ....

Address ....

....